W9-BGD-264

HUNTER OF
THE BLOOD

HUNTER OF THE BLOOD

A NOVEL OF SUSPENSE

Whit Masterson

DODD, MEAD & COMPANY, NEW YORK

Copyright © 1977 by Whit Masterson
All rights reserved
No part of this book may be reproduced in any form
without permission in writing from the publisher
Printed in the United States of America
by The Haddon Craftsmen, Inc., Scranton, Penna.

1 2 3 4 5 6 7 8 9 10

Library of Congress Cataloging in Publication Data

Masterson, Whit, pseud.
  Hunter of the blood.

  I. Title.
PZ4.M414Hu [PS3563.A835] 813'.5'4 76–58518
ISBN 0–396–07417–0

To ED SIEVERS
A great photographer, an even greater friend

WHILE EVERYONE AGREES that an ounce of prevention is worth a pound of cure and that a stitch in time saves nine and so forth and so on, there is something about prevention which interests everyone less than cures or attempted cures. There is some kind of curious resistance in all of us to the idea of preventing anything and we act only when we are forced to do so. And sometimes not even then.

—*Karl Menninger*

Contents

The
Shambles

THE UBO TRIBESMEN of the southern Philippines are skilled hunters, a necessity in a region where game is not abundant. Trained from birth in the mysteries of the chase, the Ubo do not consider their talent remarkable, as an outsider might. Occasionally, however, there emerges a man with an exceptional gift, able to discern a trail which others cannot and to follow it, often for great distances, led by little save what we might call intuition. The Ubo have no equivalent word in their vocabulary. They claim instead that such a hunter has a peculiar affinity with his quarry, that he is able to detect its heartbeat and to scent the blood coursing through its veins. The name they give him is dugô mañgañgaso, hunter of the blood.

Civilized man, while remaining a hunter, has scant use for this talent. He stalks his quarry—whether animal or fish or fellow man—by more sophisticated means and, surely, the aircraft and the satellite, the radio and the radar and the

1

computer, are far more reliable than human intuition. There is no question about it, no question at all. But still, and on the other hand . . .

Southern California's Mojave is high desert. Like the low deserts, it is searingly hot in summer. Unlike them, it can be excruciatingly cold in winter, and snow is not uncommon. On this evening in early March there was no snow. The last measurable precipitation had fallen a week earlier and the thirsty soil had long since swallowed it. But a chilling wind, born in the far-off Arctic Circle, was gusting across the bleak plateau. The temperature stood in the low forties. On such a night only the hardiest of predators prowled the darkness in search of prey. Most sought the comfort of nests and burrows.

However, there were exceptions. The two men in the armored truck were neither predators nor (to the best of their knowledge) prey. They moved across the frigid wasteland not in search of food but for a reason unknown to the lower animals: They were being paid to do so. They experienced no discomfort save ennui. The wind clawed at the climate-controlled cab in which they rode, but could not penetrate it. They grumbled not at the harshness of Mother Nature but at the restrictions of other men.

"Wish to hell they'd let us use the good road," Fred Towler complained, jerking his head toward the north where, a mile distant, the broad freeway glowed with the headlights of the pleasure-seekers for whom it had been constructed, rushing toward Las Vegas. "Or at least knock off this forty miles an hour crap."

"You know the reasons," the driver reproved. His voice fell into a singsong as he chanted the offending regulation. " 'To provide for public safety in the event of an accident—' "

"Public safety, hell. Public relations, you mean. They're scared that some chicken heart would squawk if it got around that . . . How long you been making this run, Ira? Ten years, anyway."

"More like twelve."

"In all that time has there ever been an accident? Has there even been a close call?"

Ira Yontis regarded his partner tolerantly. He was by far the senior of the pair, not only in service but in age. He was nearly fifty, Towler barely thirty. Though privately he might consider the regulations overly strict, he lived comfortably within their framework. "What's eating you, sonny? Tonight's no different than any other night."

"We could make this run in five hours if they'd let us, instead of taking damn near all night."

"At least, you've got good company. Or are you trying to tell me that you don't love me any more?"

"I'm trying to tell you that I got something better to do with my nights than spending them with an old goat like you."

"That broad in Vegas, maybe? Name one thing she can do that I can't. Okay, so there's one. Name two."

Towler chuckled unwillingly. "She's not just another broad, Ira. She's something special. I might even marry her."

"Don't be a chump. Take it from a guy who's been down that road—not just once, three times. I guarantee you'll find it a lot rougher than this one." He gestured at the narrow ribbon of concrete which stretched out before their headlights, seemingly to infinity. "You got a good thing going, Fred. Soft job, high pay and nobody to tell you how to spend it. Why do you want to go and louse it up?"

"Ever heard of a little thing called love?"

"You're not talking about love. You're talking about marriage. If you're smart, you'll grab all you can get of the first and forget about the other. I wish somebody had told me that thirty years ago."

"The trouble with you, Ira, is that you never found the right girl."

"You're like those suckers at the crap tables on the Strip. They know damn well it's a house game, but they keep right on playing just the same. And sooner or later they all seven out." Though he spoke with conviction, Yontis was not actually trying to sway the younger man. It was merely a subject for conversation, one not hitherto exhausted, to relieve the tedium of the long drive. "So you think you've found the right girl, huh? What makes you so sure? How long you known her, anyway?"

"Long enough."

"I figure no more than a couple of months," Yontis estimated judiciously. "And half that time you've been on the road." He sensed that he had struck a sore spot and could not resist prodding it. "How does she spend all those lonely hours while you're away? Where is she right now, for instance? I'll bet you don't have the foggiest."

"Wrong. I know exactly where she is. She doesn't get off work till one A.M."

"And I suppose she trots right on home like a good little girl and cries herself to sleep with your picture. Sure, she does."

"Knock it off, Ira," Towler advised thinly. "You don't know her and I do and I know damn well I can trust her. We made a date for breakfast—just as soon as I finish the run and check out. Would she do that if she was playing around with some other guy?"

"Depends on how big an appetite she's got." He saw from Towler's angry profile that he had carried his needling far enough, and perhaps farther. "Just funning, old buddy. Go

4

ahead and marry the girl if that's what you want. Who knows? You might be one of the lucky ones." To change the subject, he asked, "What time is it, anyhow?"

"Nearly midnight. Better check in with Mother, I guess." Towler turned on the shortwave radio. He grinned at Yontis, his normal good nature reasserting itself. "Watch me shake 'em up a little." He spoke into the microphone. "For the third and last time. This is NMC 319 calling Maverick Mesa. Come in, please."

A voice replied immediately, "This is Maverick Mesa acknowledging. 319, we did not receive your previous transmissions. Suggest you check for mechanical malfunction and use alternate frequency if necessary."

"This is the alternate frequency, Charlie. Suggest you stop reading those comic books and pay attention to your job."

"Very funny." Charlie's sigh could be felt rather than heard. "You got any real problems, Towler—besides that so-called sense of humor?"

"You bet. We're surrounded by Indians and running out of ammunition. What are our instructions?"

"Play it straight, won't you?" the operator begged. "What's your present position and ETA?"

"Your wife is right, Charlie. You're no fun at all." Towler glanced at the odometer and made a quick calculation. "Okay, we're seventy-four miles out and holding to assigned route and speed. Estimating Maverick Mesa at 0135 hours."

"Roger, 319," Charlie replied in a now-that's-better tone. "We have you logged at minus seventy-four, condition green. Your final check will be in fifty-eight minutes."

Yontis, though amused by his partner's clowning, felt that seniority carried the responsibility to admonish mildly. "You'll be sorry if the boss just happened to be monitoring that transmission."

"So I bring a little excitement into his dull drab life."

5

Towler shrugged, unconcerned. "Anyway, we both know that nobody ever monitors our transmissions."

"One of these times, somebody will," Yontis warned. Yet he did not take his own prophecy seriously. There was no way he could have known that it had already been fulfilled.

The Maverick Mesa communications officer aroused K. K. Hartman from a sound sleep at two A.M. to advise him that NMC 319 had failed to log in on schedule. Repeated efforts had failed to raise it; the initial assumption was that the truck had suffered a radio malfunction. Now, however, 319 was thirty minutes overdue and the communications officer felt that the base administrator should be informed.

Hartman, a phlegmatic man, was concerned but not unduly alarmed. "Probably had engine trouble or blew a tire."

"Yes, sir. But why haven't they informed us?"

"You said it yourself. Radio malfunction. It wouldn't be the first time." He yawned. "Better send out a car to find them—and to give them a tow if they need it. Keep me posted."

He went back to bed. And back to sleep. His job demanded that he deal constantly with problems, most of them greater than an overdue truck, and experience taught that the majority solved themselves.

At four-thirty, Hartman was awakened once more. The reconnaissance car had traveled the road all the way to Barstow and back again. There was no sign of NMC 319. Could the truck have chosen an alternate route? Highly unlikely; judging from its last reported position, there was no alternate route available to it. Could the truck have pulled off the road, far enough so that the recon had failed to spy it in the darkness? Possible—but if so, why?

"Good question." And one which Hartman could not answer. "Well, contact the California Highway Patrol and the San Bernardino sheriff's department, find out if they know something we don't. If the answer's no, tell Elkin to get the chopper ready. I'll take a look as soon as there's enough light to see by."

Sunrise came a few minutes before seven. The sun had not yet cleared the eastern horizon when Hartman, all other avenues exhausted, was airborne. Stanley Elkin, the base pilot, was at the controls of the two-seat Bell 47-G helicopter. They turned west toward the nearby California border. Below them, the rising sun painted the desert a soft pink that rapidly faded into a mottled gray.

Hartman nudged his companion. "There's the old road, Stan. Stay with it. If 319 is anywhere on this damn desert, we'll spot it."

"What could have happened to it, K.K.?"

"If I knew, I'd still be in bed, where I belong."

The two men studied the monotonous landscape unrolling beneath them. Much of it was bare, too arid to support even cacti. The rocky soil was laced with sandy arroyos in which water occasionally flowed. Near them grew the hardy chaparral, mesquite and sage and Russian thistle, and here and there reared up tall Joshua trees like lonely sentinels. Man had left his mark upon the desert in the form of infrequent side roads, little more than trails, which branched off the highway toward God knew where. Hartman used binoculars to study each. None showed any evidence of recent use.

"Damn it, they've got to be here," he muttered.

The minutes and the miles continued to roll by. Hartman, his uneasiness growing, began a slow sweep of the horizon. "Hey, I think I saw something! Just a flash of light—about five miles ahead on the port side. Yeah, there it is again. Could be a reflection off a windshield."

Elkin increased their speed. The wink of light was not repeated since the angle of observation had changed. But, before long, Hartman was able to verify its source. "It's 319, all right!"

"You sure?

"I can read the numbers on the roof." The armored truck stood in the middle of a shallow arroyo, hidden by the contour of the earth from the nearby highway but plainly visible from the air. He sucked in his breath. "Oh-oh."

"What's wrong?"

"Don't know yet. Something looks screwy. Set this bird down, Stan. Anywhere—but make it fast!"

They passed over the ominously silent truck. Elkin, choosing a clear and level spot east of the arroyo, brought the craft rapidly to earth. Both men were out of the cockpit before the rotor blades stopped turning.

They scrambled down the brush-choked slope and ran toward the armored truck, shoes sinking in the soft sand. All at once they halted, as if responding to some unspoken command, and stood frozen in place, staring, with only the rasp of their labored breathing disturbing the silence.

The truck's windshield, constructed to withstand the impact of a .45-caliber bullet at point-blank range, had been pierced as though it were facial tissue. Of the glass, some fragments had survived intact; though shattered, it was still identifiable as a windshield. Of the two men it was designed to protect, little recognizable remained. Once past the glass barrier, the projectile had literally torn them to bits. One gloved hand, minus any arm, still gripped the crumpled steering wheel. On the ledge behind the seat lay a blackened something that could have been a human head. The explosion had touched off a searing fire, turning the cab into an inferno. The fire was gone but its smell remained, an aroma of charred fabric and scorched metal and roasted flesh.

Elkin spun away, retching. Hartman, mastering his own nausea, attempted to wrest open the cab door, as though by

8

reaching the men inside he still might save them. But the door lock held and at last, realizing the futility of his efforts, he staggered back a few paces and stood regarding the carnage with impotent anger.

"Why would anyone do a thing like this?" Elkin asked in a choked voice.

"To keep Ira and Frank from hitting the security button, give them no chance to activate the distress emergency signal."

"But why?" Elkin implored. "They still couldn't get to the cargo."

Hartman stared at him for a moment. "That's right," he agreed in a whisper. "It's been tested a dozen times . . ." But there was no certainty in his voice. He whirled suddenly and ran to the rear of the vehicle.

The massive truck, developed at a cost exceeding $100,000, was constructed of steel alloys which a drill could not puncture and a welder's torch could not cut. The doors to the storage room locked with an electronically encoded combination. And, should they be forced in some fashion, the attempt activated a spray of anesthetizing gas—while at the same time a rapidly hardening synthetic foam formed an impenetrable shield over the cargo. These features had caused those who built it and those who operated it to call NMC 319 the world's most secure truck.

The boast now stood revealed as hollow. A second explosive had blasted the heavy door free of its hinges, exposing the cavernous storage room. The anesthetizing gas had long since dissipated without accomplishing its intended purpose. The synthetic foam, the last of the vaunted fail-safe devices, had apparently lived up to specifications, hardening to a rocklike consistency within three minutes.

But obviously three minutes had proved too long. The cargo which it had been designed to shield, twenty kilograms

9

of plutonium oxide—more valuable than gold and far more deadly—was gone.

The Maverick Mesa Nuclear Fuels Facility, which had been NMC 319's destination, occupied a remote corner of the atomic proving grounds northwest of Las Vegas. At night the lights of the Nevada resort city could be distinguished on the horizon. But few of the tourists who thronged the casinos and luxury hotels were aware of Maverick Mesa's existence, and fewer still had ever seen it. Those who, through error or curiosity, followed the little-traveled road to its terminus usually returned with no clear knowledge of what lay on the other side of the high chain-link fence.

Which was precisely as the Nuclear Regulatory Commission—successor to the Atomic Energy Commission—intended. The site had been chosen in large measure for its low visibility quotient, isolated from the population centers its product was intended to serve, but not excessively remote from them. Painful experience had taught that, where nuclear materials were concerned, public knowledge inevitably translated into public alarm. Never mind the safeguards installed; the argument that "We've got to put the plant somewhere" was invariably answered with "That's fine—but put it somewhere else." So if the NRC did not precisely conceal Maverick Mesa's existence, still it did its best to avoid advertising the fact. Even the signs which warned the uninvited visitor against trespass merely advised that he had illegally entered a U.S. government reservation.

Maverick Mesa's function, and its reason for being, was to supply the needs of the nuclear breeder reactors, both federal and private, whose number increased year by year. Here the man-made element plutonium-239—which was rapidly replacing uranium as a reactor fuel—was processed, fabricated into fuel rods and shipped to the nuclear installations . . . and returned later in the form of plutonium oxide for recycling. It was a continuous circle from plant to reactor and back to plant again in which the plutonium—familiarly called ploot —was used, transmuted but never exhausted; the breeders actually produced more fuel than they consumed.

Now, for the first time, the circle had been broken.

Twenty kilograms, or roughly forty-four pounds, of ploot, bound for Maverick Mesa from the nuclear power generating station on the Southern California coast at Punta Fierro, were missing and presumed stolen . . . but by whom and for what purpose only those responsible as yet knew.

The
Hunter

THE XANADU was nearly ten years old and could no longer claim to be the newest of the resort hotels on the Las Vegas Strip. But it was still among the largest and most luxurious, and its lavishly appointed casino—for which all else existed —remained unsurpassed. Like most, it operated full-blast twenty-four hours of every day. Although it was now four-thirty on a Monday morning, the big room was nearly as crowded as if it were instead Saturday evening, and only a newcomer considered it strange.

Gus Gamble shuffled the cards expertly, showed the top card and placed it face up on the bottom of the deck. He dealt two cards, one up and one down, to the three players who faced him across the crescent-shaped table. He gave himself the same number and looked expectantly at the player on his left.

She was a motherly woman of sixty-plus with snow-white hair piled atop her head and sequined spectacles perched

12

halfway down the bridge of her nose. Gamble, whose habit was to assign mental nicknames to his otherwise anonymous opponents, thought of her as Sun City Sue. She had a nine showing. She looked from it at Gamble's six, peeked again at her hole card and hesitated, crimson lips pursed, while she performed some silent computation. "Stand," she decided finally.

The man beside her—Chopin—was a paunchy pianist from the hotel's lounge. His nightly gig ended at two A.M.; he usually unwound by returning some and occasionally all of his earnings to his employers in the casino. Tonight, however, he was slightly ahead. "Hit me easy," he invited. Gamble obliged with a five. Chopin grinned and placed his ten-dollar bet on top of his cards. Gamble swung slightly on his stool to face the third player.

He had begun by dubbing the young man Sonny in deference to his age, which was about twenty-five. Shortly, he substituted Sucker in acknowledgement of his card sense, which was scanty. He proved once more that he merited the derogatory nickname by turning up his hole card. "Splitting fives."

Gamble concealed his sigh of pity. Beating the house at blackjack was difficult enough even when you played the percentages. The youngster had either never heard of them or—like many novices—supposed that he might flout them with impunity. He had been playing for nearly two hours. As so often happens, he began by winning big on two successive blackjacks (which, significantly, requires no expertise whatever). He had long since dissipated his winnings and a goodly portion of his capital as well. From his increasingly desperate expression and ever more reckless attempts to recoup, Gamble suspected that it was money he could not afford to lose.

Another hundred of Sucker's dollars changed hands when, as the oddsmakers predict, splitting the fives resulted in a

13

double disaster. Chopin won with nineteen. Sun City Sue, standing on sixteen, lost to Gamble's seventeen. She took her defeat with good grace. Not so Sucker; he cursed his luck vehemently.

Chopin, money ahead, yawned and decided aloud that he'd had enough. Gamble suggested softly, "Maybe you should pack it in too, son. This doesn't seem to be your night."

Sucker regarded him with surprise. "Isn't my money any good all of a sudden?"

"It's as good as it ever was. I'd just like to see you keep a little of it."

The warning aroused only antagonism. "Don't worry about me. I'm about due to bust this game wide open."

Gamble dealt the next hand. Sue won with twenty. Gamble and the young man pushed, both holding eighteen. "What'd I tell you?" Sucker exclaimed. "My luck's turned."

"Not losing isn't the same thing as winning."

"Hey, what's with you, anyway? You've been taking my money for the last couple of hours. Now you're trying to get me to quit before I have a chance to get even."

"Just a piece of friendly advice. You're never going to get even. Not in this town."

"Well, I'll be damned!" Like all suckers, he didn't care to face the truth. "I've played in a lot bigger games than this, buddy. But this is the first time I ever met a smart ass dealer like you. I got a good mind to report you. I'll bet your boss wouldn't go for your kind of crap."

Gamble smiled. "That's another bet you'd lose. The boss doesn't like to send anybody away flat broke. It's bad for you, bad for him. I'm just trying to give you both a break."

"Yeah? All you give me is a pain in the ass." He shoved back from the table. "You and this whole lousy dump."

"If the pain gets too intense, look me up. I might have the

14

antidote. My name's Gamble. That should be easy for you to remember."

The young man stamped away without deigning to reply. Sun City Sue asked curiously, "Are you going to send me away too, Mr. Gamble? I'm not winning, either."

"You're not losing more than you can afford. He was. You know when to quit without being told. He doesn't."

"Don't you suppose he'll just go to another casino?"

"Could be. And then, maybe the cold night air will change his mind and he'll go home where he belongs."

She tittered. "Well, he was certainly right about one thing. I've been coming to Vegas for years—and you're like no other dealer I ever met."

"You can say that again, honey," a new voice agreed. It belonged to a plump balding man, the casino's pit boss, who had arrived in time to overhear the woman's remark but not what had prompted it. However, he was able to hazard a shrewd guess. "You up to your old tricks, Gus?"

"The gentleman who just left thinks you should fire me, Arnold."

"My pleasure. Just be here tomorrow night at the regular time so I can rehire you." He nudged Gamble with his elbow. "Move the bod."

Gamble glanced at his wristwatch; the casino, in keeping with Las Vegas practice, had no clock of its own. "I've got nearly an hour to go."

"You don't listen too good. You're fired. Actually, there's a gent upstairs who claims he's in need of your services."

"Oh? What's his problem?"

"He didn't say—and I know better than to ask." Arnold slid onto the vacated stool. "Room 1011. He didn't sound like a jumper. But I've been wrong before, so get the lead out."

"Want to cash me in?"

15

"Hell, no. If I can't trust you, who can I trust?"

In the employees' basement lounge, Gamble exchanged the brocaded jacket all the dealers wore for his own suit coat. As the service elevator bore him swiftly upward, he wondered who had seen fit to summon him and for what purpose. If Arnold were to be believed, the call was urgent. Mentally, he reviewed all those with whom he had come in contact recently. None rang a bell. Except possibly the young man he had nicknamed Sucker, and it was too early yet to hear from him, if indeed he ever did. Well, it was probably a stranger.

In contrast to the bustling casino below, the floors above were somnolent; even the early risers were not astir. Gamble found Room 1011 and knocked lightly. He was expected. Almost immediately, the latch clicked and the door swung open.

The face which peered at him did not belong to a stranger, after all, although it had been several years since Gamble had last seen it. Then it had usually been stern and frequently scowling. Now it wore a smile of anticipation.

"Gus!" its owner exclaimed. "Gus Gamble!" And then he checked. "Or should I call you Father?"

"Only if you want me to hear your confession." Gamble grinned. "And since that's highly unlikely, you can call me anything you like, General."

His full name was Ashley Ainsworth Womack, but few save his parents had ever employed it. To his contemporaries, he was A.A.; to his family, Ash. Gamble, who belonged in neither group, had always called him General, prompted by respect rather than regulations, since their association was not service-connected. Womack had doffed the Army's uniform more than a decade ago. Gamble had known him only as the then Atomic Energy Commission's chief executive

16

officer. But Womack retained the crisp bearing, the authoritative manner, that far more than insignia marks the West Pointer. At sixty-seven, the stocky figure was still ramrod straight and weighed less than its cadet days. The bullet head was no balder than Gamble remembered. Only a blurring, a softening of the once sharply chiseled features and a slight palsy suggested that Ashley Womack was in the twilight of a second distinguished (and, no doubt, final) career.

The hand with which he drew Gamble into the room was still muscular. "Thanks for coming—particularly at this ridiculous hour of the morning."

"I'm used to ridiculous hours, General. It's a psychological fact that the human spirit is at its lowest ebb about four A.M. That's why I prefer to work the graveyard shift."

"Well, your spirit seems to be doing all right," Womack appraised. "The life must agree with you. How old are you now, Gus? Forty-four? Damned if you couldn't pass for thirty-four."

Womack was indulging in kindly exaggeration, of course, as friends invariably do. But he was not exaggerating greatly as friends sometimes do. Gamble's abundant black hair and bushy mustache were untinged by gray. His swarthy face with its prominent hooked nose and deep-set pale blue eyes retained much of the youthful raffishness which certain women had found more disturbing than good looks. His body had changed the most, yet in a way not immediately apparent. Since the accident, he was an inch shorter due to the compression of certain spinal vertebrae and the surgical fusion which made it permanent. But because he still stood nearly six feet in height, only he and his tailor were aware of the diminishment.

"I was about to have a snort when you got here, Gus. I don't suppose I could prevail on you to join me—even though you're out of uniform."

17

"Why not? My provincial has a weakness for martinis himself."

"Your provincial?"

"Jesuit jargon. Corresponds roughly to bishop."

Womack poured two glasses. "It's a strange world," he murmured. "I don't know which amazes me more. To find my old hardnosed chief of internal security as a Jesuit priest. Or to find a priest dealing blackjack in a Las Vegas casino."

"It's a peculiar parish, all right," Gamble agreed. "But the action isn't in the churches these days. It's in the streets. That's where people are hurting. Especially here in Vegas. They don't need sermons, they need help. So I run a spiritual pushcart up and down the Strip."

"That much I can understand. It's the dealer bit that boggles my mind."

"If I wear the clerical collar and a black suit, I turn off the people I'm trying to reach. But put me behind a table in a fancy jacket and a red satin tie and I meet them on their own level. That way, I'm able to minister to them."

"How?" Womack asked curiously. "Confessions behind the slot machines—that sort of thing?"

Gamble shrugged. "Different strokes for different folks. I furnish a friendly face they can rap with or a shoulder to cry on—or a kick in the rump if that's what they need."

"How in the world did you ever con the casino into cooperating with you? The operators never struck me as a bunch of do-gooders."

"I knew the Xanadu's top man from the days when I operated the AEC's aerial surveillance unit out of McCarran Field. He wasn't too jazzed with my proposition at first but I talked him into it."

"You always were hard to discourage once you made up your mind," Womack recalled with a smile. "I wish I could have heard your pitch. It must have been a classic."

"The first couple of months I was treated like some kind of freak. Then, as the word got around, they began to realize that having a resident padre was good public relations. Pretty soon I started getting offers from the other casinos. The Xanadu's still my home base, but now I've got shills all over town—dealers, bartenders, waitresses, bellhops—who steer the sinners to me." He grinned. "My act's a smash, General. I'm thinking of asking for billing."

"Do you ever miss your old life?"

Gamble shook his head quickly. "I don't look back."

"I guess I didn't really believe you were serious when you quit. I thought for sure that you'd come back to us as soon as you shook off the effects of the accident."

"Some effects you don't shake off easily. My spine mended, more or less, but . . . You ever spend six months flat on your back in a hospital? It gives you plenty of time to think. At first I was just grateful to be alive. Then I began asking myself why. Why was I the only one, out of one hundred and thirty-nine people aboard that 707, to survive? It wasn't that I deserved it more than they. There were better human beings on that flight. The only answer I could come up with was that God had put his finger on me for some reason."

Womack shifted in his chair as though embarrassed by the explanation. "What makes you so sure there is an answer—except maybe chance? These things happen all the time, Gus. I've seen plenty of damn good men die for no better reason than that they were in the wrong place at the wrong time . . . and worse men survive because they weren't. If there is a heavenly plan operating, it sure as hell doesn't make sense to me."

"Relax, you old agnostic," Gamble told him with a smile. "I'm not trying to convert you. I'm simply telling you how it was with me—and only because you asked. The bottom line is that I finally said, 'Okay, God, if you have given me

19

a second chance, what do you want me to do with it?' "

"You make it sound like you'd led a wasted life up till then," Womack objected. "I know better. I was there. You had a lot to be proud of. Barely thirty, and running one of the biggest security operations in the country. And running it better than anybody before or since, too."

"Sure, I was pretty good and I knew it. But I was replaceable and I knew that, too. My job existed before I got there and it went right on existing after I left. I wanted to put the rest of my life—my second life—into doing something that maybe wouldn't get done at all if I didn't do it."

"But why become a priest? No offense intended, Gus, but it strikes me as a pretty pallid occupation for a man with your talents."

Gamble was silent for a moment. "There was an old Jesuit missionary in the same room with me. He was dying and I wasn't—but I've never known anyone with such an inner joy. I guess you could call his life pallid compared to mine. But he had something I didn't, a sense of fulfillment. I wanted that kind of fulfillment for myself."

"And have you gotten it?" Womack inquired shrewdly.

"I'm working on it." Gamble drained his glass. "That's enough about me. What's your problem, General?"

"What makes you think I have a problem?"

"For one thing, you were never big on idle conversation, especially at five in the morning. For another, you've had plenty of chances to look me up and you haven't bothered till now. Finally, you've been buttering me up—and that's not your style unless you want something."

Womack grunted. "There's still a lot of cop in you. Okay, I confess. I have a reason for wanting to talk to you." He hesitated. "Do you happen to remember something called the Sigma Scenario?"

"Of course. I wrote it."

"I know you wrote it—but it's been a while. How much of it do you recall?"

Gamble rubbed his chin reflectively. "It was a forward projection of the security problems AEC was likely to face when the plutonium-fueled reactors went into operation. I postulated that the proliferation of ploot would pose a danger greater than any we'd faced before. Its high yield ratio and its relatively low radioactivity—combined with the fact that it could be easily transported—would make it an extremely attractive target for terrorists or political radicals. The Sigma Scenario was an attempt to dramatize what I considered the most likely methods they might employ to get their hands on the ploot. That's about it, General. Do I pass?"

"Not yet. Be a little more specific."

"Well, the way I saw it, we were most vulnerable to attack during the time when the plutonium oxide was being returned from the reactor to the plant for reprocessing. I suggested that a well-armed and well-organized gang wouldn't have a great deal of trouble knocking off one of our trucks. As an example, I used the Punta Fierro to Maverick Mesa run with its long exposed route across the . . ." He broke off, his gaze suddenly horrified. "Good Lord! Is that your problem, General?"

"Yeah," Womack agreed heavily. "Except that it's not just my problem, Gus. As of one week ago tonight, it's everybody's problem."

And now it was Womack's turn to talk and Gamble's turn to listen. When he had heard it all, he could not restrain his indignation. "Where was your security, anyway? My scenario recommended specific measures to prevent such a thing from ever happening. More guards, convoys instead of single vehicle shipments, armored cars instead of ordinary

21

trucks . . . Do you mean to tell me that none of them was ever implemented?"

"For a while, yes. Then last year ERDA came up with this fancy new truck, the last word in security, guaranteed hijack-proof. Trouble is, I believed them. We're spending close to one hundred million bucks a year on security. So when they told me to cut the budget, I figured that, with this new truck, we could lay off some of the other security measures."

"In other words, the *Titanic* syndrome. The ship can't possibly sink, so never mind carrying enough lifeboats."

"During the last six years, we've had two hundred and twenty-three threats or attempted acts of violence against our nuclear installations. Our security took care of every one without even raising a sweat. I guess that made us overconfi-dent."

"All winning streaks come to an end, General. Just ask me. I see it happen every night."

"This is a bet we can't afford to lose, Gus. We're talking about maybe a hundred thousand lives. My people tell me that we've got another week, two at the most, before the hijackers have their bomb. The way things are going, that won't be long enough by a damn sight."

He looked so dejected that Gamble put aside further re-proach; Womack already bore a heavy burden of guilt. "It's still early in the game. You'll get a handle on it."

"That's what I've been telling the White House. I wish I had some reason to believe it. I've never felt so helpless. I've fought in two wars, been in some mighty tough spots, but nothing compares to this. We could lose an entire city, maybe more." He shuddered. "I keep asking myself why the hell we ever got into this nuclear power business in the first place."

"That question comes about twenty-five years too late, General. I don't think any of us understood what sort of

22

Pandora's box we were unlocking. But we did unlock it. Now it's up to you to put the lid back on somehow."

"If we can," Womack agreed glumly.

"You must. There's simply no acceptable alternative."

"What makes it harder, Gus, is that we're working under a terrible handicap. We've got to mount the biggest manhunt in history—and without letting the public know that we're doing it. We can't enlist their help to find the hijackers. If the story gets out, there'll be a panic like nobody's ever seen before. We can't even let the local law in on it."

"And yet you're letting me in on it," Gamble murmured. "How come?"

"Haven't you guessed? I want you to come back to work for me. On a temporary basis, of course."

Gamble laughed incredulously. "That's ridiculous and you know it."

"I know nothing of the sort. Sure, it's unusual but we're facing an unusual situation. If anyone can bail us out, it's you. You wrote the Sigma Scenario, didn't you? When K. K. Hartman told me you were here in Vegas, it was like the answer to my prayer."

"I'm flattered, General. But just because I pointed out the danger before it happened doesn't mean that I can solve it now that it has. I've been out of the profession for a long time."

"It's like riding a bicycle," Womack argued. "Once you learn, you never forget. You were the best security man in the business, bar none. You weren't just smart, you were brilliant. You had a feel for it, an intuition that was positively uncanny."

"That was a long, long time ago. I might still be able to ride the bicycle but I doubt if I could win any races on it. I'll be glad to assist you with advice—"

"I don't want advice, Gus. I want you."

23

"I'm spoken for, General. Just because you can't see the collar doesn't mean it isn't there."

"I've already talked with your—what'd you call him?—your provincial. He's agreed to grant you a leave of absence."

Gamble stared. "How'd you manage that?"

"Father Frank was my division chaplain in Normandy."

"But what about your own people? Who's your chief of security now?"

"A chap named Neff, Kenneth Neff. You don't know him, he's only been with us for a couple of years. Kenny's a young eager beaver—but he's no Gus Gamble. He knows the words but he hasn't got the tune, not yet. He's never had to deal with anything as big as this hijacking."

"What makes you think he can't? Neff must have something on the ball or he wouldn't have the job."

"You want to know what his first reaction was? That the hijackers were Soviet agents. Utter nonsense, of course. The Russians have their own ploot. They'd never risk starting a war just to steal twenty kilos of ours. Neff should know that as well as I. But every man's a prisoner of his prejudices to some extent. He came to us from the CIA—and so, naturally, he sees the Commies' hand in everything. It's hard to put complete confidence in a man like that. Especially at a time like this."

"In that case, you should have fired him long before now."

"Ever hear of politics? Kenny's got the right connections. His uncle's a Senator, chairman of the Atomic Energy Committee. I'm not sure I could have fired him even if he'd given me any real cause to—which he hasn't."

"Then what makes you think you can fire him now?"

"I'm not firing him," Womack explained with a thin smile. "I'm merely bringing in a highly qualified expert to oversee the operation. Who could object to that?"

24

"Neff, for one. It amounts to a vote of no confidence and he's bound to resent it. That's human nature. Nobody appreciates an outsider—no matter how highly qualified—taking over a job that is rightfully his."

"Sure, you're not likely to win any popularity contest," Womack admitted. "But that never used to bother you. And you never shied away from a job that needed doing, either, simply because it promised to be tough."

"Maybe I've changed. People do."

"You haven't changed that much or you wouldn't be here plowing a hard furrow like Las Vegas. There must be a lot easier parishes."

"That's just the point. This is my responsibility now."

"You're copping out," Womack said with sudden harshness. "Don't bother me, I gave at the office. How can you be so damn sure what your responsibility is? And where it ends? You told me that you believe your life was spared for a purpose. Now I'm not a religious man, as you know. I'm not convinced that there is a God. Or, if there is, that he takes the slightest interest in you and me. But let's suppose I'm wrong. Let's suppose that God in his inscrutable wisdom did have some reason for bringing you out of the plane crash in one piece. Are you going to claim that consoling a few pitiful refugees from the crap tables was all he had in mind—and that you shouldn't bother to lift a finger to save maybe a hundred thousand other innocent men and women and kids? That you, with your special talent, should turn your back on them? If you can say yes and still live with yourself . . . well, all I can say is: What the hell kind of priest are you, anyway?"

Gamble started to reply, then hesitated. His eyes fell before Womack's accusing stare. He got to his feet and paced to the window. The blackness of night was turning slowly to gray as a new day was born. At last, he turned to face the other man. His smile was as wan as the eastern sky.

"You sure know how to hurt a guy," he said huskily.

The five hundred acres which comprised the Maverick Mesa Nuclear Fuels Facility were enclosed by a chain-link fence and contained a score of buildings, grouped in two distinct and widely separated clusters. The structures in the first cluster were fewer in number but larger in size. Behind their low windowless cinder block walls and beneath their corrugated steel roofs, the nuclear material was processed, fabricated and, when necessary, stored. The second cluster was less forbidding in appearance, lacking the former's grim uniformity. These buildings, some two stories in height, were constructed of wood with shingled roofs and shutters at the windows. They were designed to serve the needs of men rather than the requirements of manufacture. In them Maverick Mesa's civilian garrison ate, slept and found recreation. Although they were not compelled to live on the base, most chose to do so, opting for the convenience of the "company town" in preference to making the daily sixty-mile round trip to Las Vegas.

Between the two clusters lay several hundred yards of open ground which was intended as a buffer zone in case of a nuclear accident. However, no accident had occurred during the twenty years of Maverick Mesa's existence and so the original purpose was now largely forgotten. Part of the buffer zone had been turned, little by little, into a parking lot for the employees' automobiles and much of the remainder was occupied by a softball diamond.

The area now served a third purpose, as a temporary holding area for Nuclear Materials Carrier 319. The ravaged truck had arrived not under its own power but concealed in the gut of a huge trailer. The two bodies had been removed

26

for burial. The rest remained under armed guard—a classic example, Gamble thought, of locking the barn door after the horse was stolen.

"Seen enough?" inquired Kenneth Neff. At Gamble's nod, he ordered the trailer secured once more and led the way to the golf cart which had brought them from the main gate.

"I don't suppose the hijackers left any prints." It was not actually a question; he already assumed the answer.

"They didn't leave a damn thing," Neff confirmed. "Except four California Highway Department sawhorses and a detour sign."

Neff was in his late thirties, a tall athletic man with a shock of unruly brown hair and bluntly handsome features. Some claimed to be reminded of the late President Kennedy; others suggested that Neff cultivated the resemblance deliberately, even to the Back Bay accent. Be that as it might, Neff did not lack for identity of his own. His manner was forceful, his speech crisp. He radiated a restless energy which awed his subordinates and made his superiors uneasy. If men wore labels, Gamble suspected that Kenneth Neff's would read Don't Get in My Way.

"They had it planned to a fare-thee-well," Neff continued. "Towler and Yontis came around a bend in the road and there was the barricade. They did the natural thing. They put on the brakes. Soon as they did, the hijackers blasted them with a cannon, some sort of antitank gun with an armor-piercing shell. That was it for Towler and Yontis. They never had a chance to hit the alarm button. Then the truck was hauled or pushed off the road into a gully and the gang went to work on the cargo door. It was supposed to be blast-proof. Obviously, it wasn't."

"And so the *Titanic* went down," Gamble murmured. "How do you suppose they knew so much about the truck?"

"Hell, that's no mystery. They read it in the papers. Some

27

smart-assed reporter got hold of the plans and specifications. We couldn't stop him from printing them, though God knows I tried. But everybody's so damn scared of the media these days. I was told to lay off, that it didn't really matter, anyway. I'd like to invite them to take a look at 319!"

"No use crying over spilt milk, Kenny." Gamble pursed his lips thoughtfully. "Any idea what kind of vehicle the hijackers used to haul away the ploot?"

"There were no identifiable tire tracks. It had to be something good-sized, a van or a pickup, maybe a station wagon. The ploot was packed in a steel drum, hundred gallon size, lined with lead. You couldn't put that in a passenger car."

"What was the total weight of the drum? Or do you know?"

"Approximately three hundred pounds," Neff said in an of-course-I-know voice. "If you're trying to figure how many men it took to move it, the minimum is two. And they'd have to be strong as hell. My own feeling is that there were at least four, maybe as many as six."

"Why?"

"Psychology, for one thing. The hijackers couldn't have been sure that they'd dispose of the guards as easily as they actually did. If there'd been a fight, two against two aren't attractive odds."

"Good reasoning."

Neff did not acknowledge the compliment. "By the time we found 319, it was too late to set up roadblocks. The gang already had an eight-hour head start. And since we didn't have a description of their vehicle, it wasn't any use to put out an APB—even if we dared to risk the publicity." He looked inquiringly at Gamble. "Want to go back to Hartman's office now?"

"Let's stay here a while longer," Gamble suggested. "We've got some talking to do and I'd sooner do it where we won't be interrupted."

"You're the boss," Neff said with a shrug.

"That's the first thing we've got to talk about. I think I know how you feel but let's get it out in the open. You're steamed because General Womack has pulled an old warhorse out of the barn and put him in command of this operation, right?"

"You said it, I didn't. I'm aware of your record, Gamble. You're something of a legend in our business." His tone indicated that in his lexicon that equated with has-been. "I'm sure Womack knows what he's doing."

"Like hell. You think the old man has gone bonkers. If it's any consolation, I had the same reaction."

Once again, he failed to achieve rapport. "I've been given my orders and I'll follow them," Neff told him formally. "However, since you've invited me to speak candidly . . . I do happen to believe that I'm as qualified as you to solve this case, and perhaps more so. They tell me you were tops once. They also tell me that you're a hunch player, a go-for-broke type who prefers to fly by the seat of his pants and trust in luck to get him where he's going. Well, that's not my style. I believe that police work is ninety per cent perspiration and only ten per cent inspiration—and that anyone who thinks it's the other way around is going to wind up with egg on his face."

The blunt declaration caused Gamble to smile faintly. He could not take offense at it; Neff's prickly self-esteem reminded him too strongly of the youthful Gus Gamble. "Thanks for putting your cards on the table. Now take a look at mine. Whether you like it or not, I've been given overall responsibility for this operation and I intend to exercise it. Your opinion of me doesn't matter. Until it's been demonstrated that my methods are ineffective, I'm calling the shots. Can you live with that, Kenny?"

Neff was silent for a moment. "I guess I have to," he said finally. "Because when you fumble the ball, somebody better be around to pick it up."

"Fair enough. But don't get so wrapped up fighting me that you forget who the real enemy is."

"That's uncalled for, Gamble. I may not like you, but I want to win this one as much as you do."

"Okay, what have you done so far to win it?"

Neff enumerated the steps already taken. "I alerted the Border Patrol to seize any suspicious cargo in case the hijackers try to take the ploot into Mexico. They haven't, at least not yet. I passed the same word to the Arizona, Nevada and New Mexico agricultural inspection stations. Nothing there, either. I'm in communication with the FBI regarding political revolutionaries and other terrorist groups. Ditto the Treasury Department and armed forces counterintelligence. I begged Womack to bring in the CIA, too, but the old fart vetoed it."

"He had to, Kenny. The CIA's mandate doesn't permit them to meddle in domestic matters. That's the law."

"Screw the law. Anyway, what makes him think this is a domestic matter? I'm willing to bet it isn't." He paused as if hoping that Gamble might agree. When Gamble did not, he grunted. "You too, huh? Okay, have it your way. I've run a check on our own security files for cranks, ban-the-bomb freaks, demonstrators, that sort of thing—and I've got my people investigating every likely candidate."

"Who do you have investigating your people?"

"You suggesting that this was an inside job?"

"The hijackers didn't only know how to grab the ploot. They knew exactly when and exactly where. That sounds like inside information to me. How many people had prior knowledge of the shipment, and who are they?"

NMC 319 had been placed on forty-eight-hour alert commencing at noon Sunday prior to the hijacking. In keeping with normal security procedures, the truck's exact departure time had not been disclosed to any save those with Need to Know classification. The ploot had not been loaded aboard until a half-hour before departure Monday evening and Maverick Mesa itself was not informed until 319 was already on the road. Therefore, the leak, if any, had originated at Punta Fierro—and Neff was strongly inclined to doubt that there was a leak at all.

"There were only five men who knew what time 319 was due to leave and what route it was going to take. All top echelon personnel, all with Q clearance. We don't hand that out lightly, in case you've forgotten."

Gamble decided that his patronizing manner invited humbling. "I haven't forgotten Q clearance. I haven't forgotten how to count, either. You say there were five? I say there were seven." He indicated the huge trailer with its shattered cargo. "The men who drove 319, they had to know too, didn't they?"

"Towler and Yontis?" Neff bit his lip. "Yes," he admitted grudgingly. "They knew, too. But why should they commit suicide by tipping off the hijackers?"

"Could be they didn't know they were committing suicide."

"Fred and Ira were fine men with spotless records. I can't believe that either one of them would sell out. I'd sooner suspect my own brother."

"I don't know your brother—so convince me. Was either one a drinker? A gambler? In debt? Were they having marital problems, anything like that?"

"I keep close tabs on my people—and the answer is no, right on down the line. Yontis was married a couple of times but he'd been single for at least five years. Towler was a bachelor, never been married. And, no, he wasn't gay, either.

31

He had a girl in Vegas. He told me that they were planning on getting hitched."

"How did she take it? His death, I mean."

"I don't know," Neff said. "We notified Towler's next of kin, of course, a sister back in Pennsylvania. Gave her the same story we gave the papers, that he'd been killed in a single car accident. There wasn't any reason to notify his girl, no legal reason, anyway."

"It would have been considerate, though," Gamble murmured. "But you had more important things on your mind. What's her name, by the way?"

Again Neff was forced to confess ignorance; it rankled him to do so. "I can find out."

"First things first. Right now, I think we'd better zero in on Towler and Yontis. After they went on alert at Punta Fierro, did either one of them leave the compound? Have any visitors? Write any letters? Make any phone calls? In other words, if either one of them even talked in his sleep, I want to know what he said."

"I'll get on it. If I dig up anything, you'll hear it."

"Let me hear what you dig up on me, too." Neff's guilty expression made him grin. "I'm not really a mind reader, Kenny. But you know I wrote the scenario for this hijacking. I'm sure it must have occurred to you that what we have here could be a self-fulfilling prophecy."

Neff left immediately for Punta Fierro at the controls of an Aero Commander, one of several jet aircraft which the Commission maintained. He expected his new superior to accompany him but Gamble, who had no love for airplanes and avoided them whenever possible, declined. He explained with a half-truth. "I've got some things to do here. I'll drive down to L.A. and meet you there this evening."

He lunched with K. K. Hartman in the Maverick Mesa

mess hall and from him received a vivid recapitulation of the discovery of the looted truck. The story added nothing save gruesome detail to what Gamble already knew. However, Hartman was able to provide fresh insight on the political situation.

"What Womack won't tell you is that he's hanging on by his fingernails. When the late lamented Atomic Energy Commission was split in twain, the General had to take what amounted to a demotion. Instead of running the whole show, he was left with just Nerk." The faintly sinister nickname was new to Gamble; it was how its employees referred to the Nuclear Regulatory Commission which, among other functions, was responsible for atomic security. "On top of that, he's got young Kenny Neff breathing down his neck—ready, willing and mighty anxious to take over the minute it appears that the old soldier can't hack it any longer. So Womack had two reasons for resurrecting you. The first, obviously, was to solve the case. The second, maybe not so obvious, was to save his ass. Keep the latter in mind, Gus."

"That sounds like a warning."

"A frightened man is an unreliable friend," Hartman observed cynically. "Womack will back you against Neff just as long as it's to his advantage to do so. But the minute it isn't to his advantage . . . He'll go with the winner, whoever that happens to be."

"You've got the wrong idea, K.K. I'm not competing with Neff."

"No," Hartman said shrewdly, "you're really competing with something a lot worse—your own legend. And I strongly suspect that it'd hurt like hell to have it punctured."

Later, he met with Dr. Vincent Sorbo, Maverick Mesa's chief physicist, to discuss another—and to Gamble a far more important—aspect of the problem they faced. Sorbo painted a disturbing picture.

33

"The basic question, of course, is: Can the people who hijacked the plutonium oxide come up with a workable bomb? The answer, I'm sorry to say, is yes, they can. The method for doing so is readily available. You can find it at the public library. It doesn't require any really advanced scientific or technical training. Anyone with ordinary laboratory and machine shop skills—plus a knowledge of high school algebra—could do it. In simple terms, you surround the plutonium core with a tamper and surround the tamper with chemical high explosive. When you detonate the explosive, the tamper is compressed. This in turn compresses the ploot and"—he spread his hands expressively—"boom!"

"In physical terms, how big would the bomb have to be?"

"How high is up? It could be as small as a basketball or as large as a piano. It really depends on what kind of explosive you use and how powerful you want the boom to be. To utilize twenty kilograms of ploot for maximum yield, I'd say that the bomb would have to be, oh, the size of a hot water heater at least."

"Suppose they go for the maximum—what sort of blast are we talking about?"

"Let's compare it this way. The first A-bomb, the crude one we dropped on Hiroshima, was in the same range. But that's not all of it. To the initial casualties—which could be staggering—you've got to add everyone who gets hit by the fallout. Ploot is the most toxic substance known to man. Inhaling or ingesting even a speck may cause cancer."

"So I understand."

"Do you also understand that ploot comes mighty close to being immortal? It has an HLS—hazardous life span—of four hundred and eighty thousand years. In other words, once an area is contaminated, it's contaminated forever. Or, at least, what you and I consider forever."

"You mean there's no way to clean it up?"

"Hell, we haven't even found a way to store it safely. To be honest about it, we've got a tiger by the tail and all we can do is hold on." Sorbo's smile was laced with gallows humor. "But give us a little time—a thousand years or so—and perhaps we'll have figured out how to tame the beast."

Gamble departed Maverick Mesa in late afternoon and headed west into California. The broad freeway offered the fastest route to Los Angeles but he left it to follow the old road. With Hartman's directions to guide him, he had no difficulty locating the spot where the ambush had taken place.

The area was deserted, there being no reason to place it under guard. However, it still bore ample visible evidence of the violence which had occurred there and would for some time since the desert, once scarred, is slow to heal itself. Fragments from the armored truck's windshield glistened on the highway. Trampled weeds showed where NMC 319 had been dragged or pushed off the pavement and churned sand marked the spot where it had been found. But the blood, if any, had long since been soaked up by the thirsty soil and the stench of death banished by the dry wind.

He walked about slowly, attempting to reconstruct the hijacking in his imagination. All his knowledge so far was secondhand, distilled for him by others. Now for the first time the grim picture began to come alive. By putting himself in the hijackers' place—standing where they had stood, waiting where they had waited, reliving in imagination their heart-pounding apprehension and its terrible catharsis—he was able to see them not as a faceless They but as flesh and blood men. As They, his enemies were unfathomable and, hence, unconquerable. As men, they assumed their proper proportion, comprehensible and, inevitably, fallible.

At the same time, he was conscious that he was also reliving an even more distant past—his own. Once the absorbing game of detection and pursuit had composed his entire life. He had supposed it to be over. He was surprised to find how easily he slipped back into the old role. Like a pair of shoes, stored in the attic to be rediscovered years later, the fit was still comfortable.

"Who says you can't go home again?" he murmured. "At least, for a visit."

Yet it was a homecoming which, like many, might prove to be a letdown. As Hartman had pointed out, everyone expected him to live up to his former reputation; nothing less than a miracle would do. Gamble realized that the challenge he faced was enormous. Though he termed the hijackers fallible, there was no evidence to support that belief. From beginning to end, they had mounted a well-planned and carefully executed operation in which nothing had been left behind to incriminate them.

Nothing? All at once, his heart leaped with the excitement of discovery. As he threaded his way through the thicket of mesquite which bordered the highway, his toe uncovered a small object hitherto buried in the sand. It was an empty packet of matches. Embossed in silver on the black cover were the words *Desert Sands Resort, Barstow, California.*

The crumpled folder lay too far from the road to have been thrown from a passing automobile. Someone standing in this very spot had discarded it. And recently; the packet appeared too new to have resided long in the thicket. It was possible that one of the Nerk investigators had dropped it. But since they had come from Maverick Mesa, how had any of them acquired a match folder from a resort in Barstow—which lay in the opposite direction? Suppose instead that a man crouched here in the darkness as he waited for the armored truck to appear, smoking to relieve the awful tension. . . .

NMC 319 had been placed on forty-eight-hour alert at

noon Sunday, its precise departure time known to no one. Had the hijackers gone on the same forty-eight-hour alert, poised to strike at any moment? If so, where had they spent the intervening day and a half before their target actually appeared? Not here, certainly, where their presence might be noticed and remembered later, but somewhere close by.

"I wonder how far it is to the Desert Sands Resort?" he said aloud.

The answer to his question proved to be twenty-three miles. Even with a stop in Barstow to ask directions, Gamble still covered the distance in less than three-quarters of an hour. Which, he decided, was close enough to have served as the hijackers' advance base.

The Desert Sands Resort lay northeast of the desert community at the base of low eroded hills. It was not, as he expected, a motel but a campground for trailers and recreational vehicles, several acres of sand studded with trees and laced with asphalt. Resort was perhaps too grand a name for it; however, there was a swimming pool and a snack bar and a shuffleboard court.

Karl Murach was both owner and manager. As such, he was required to be a handyman as well, and Gamble found him in the laundry room, tinkering with a recalcitrant dryer. Murach confirmed that the matches had indeed come from the Desert Sands; they were available in the office and nowhere else.

Could Murach also furnish the names of all guests who had arrived on the Sunday in question? Murach could; the registration cards were on file.

"I'm looking for a group of men traveling together," Gamble explained. "As many as five or six."

Here Murach was less helpful. Space was rented on a per-vehicle basis. The number of people in each vehicle made no difference in the fee and only the driver was required to register. Nor could he identify which, if any, of the Sunday arrivals had departed on Monday evening. Checkout time was noon. Many stayed until the last minute; others left earlier. "Some folks just pull in here for a few hours, long enough to take a shower and catch some sleep—and then they're on their way again. They pay for the full twenty-four hours, anyway, but if they don't want to use it all, I figure that's up to them."

Gamble studied the registration cards. There was a surprising number of them, nineteen in all; apparently, winter was the Desert Sands' busy season. The names, of course, meant nothing. The hijackers could not be expected to use their own. Most listed home addresses in the greater Los Angeles area with a sprinkling from central California and an even lesser number from other nearby states. Mr. and Mrs. J. Bottamiller, Allan Archer, Mrs. Sonia Wick, Mr. and Mrs. Robert Koller, Oliver Court, Gerald Couchman and family, David Johnson, Ms. Gloria Armstrong, Mr. and Mrs. Henry Moreno, E. M. Franklin . . . There was even a John Smith.

Murach recalled none of them. His guests came and went, as anonymous as shadows. Unless one created a disturbance, there was no reason to remember him. "As long as they don't bother me, I don't bother them. I'm not getting paid to stick my nose in other folks' business."

Gamble agreed that his was a lousy way to earn a living. When he returned to his car, its telephone was buzzing. Neff was on the other end of the line, calling from Punta Fierro. He had, he reported, good news—although the chagrin in his voice made it sound just the opposite.

"Well, I've been checking on Towler and Yontis. Looks like you may have lucked out, Gamble."

Score one for the hunch player. "Which one? Or was it both?"

"Fred Towler. About an hour before takeoff, he changed a five dollar bill into quarters at the payroll office. When we found his body, he had a buck and a half worth of change in his pocket. So what does that sound like to you?"

"Either he put the rest in a slot machine—or he made a phone call."

"There aren't any slots here. But there sure as hell are phones. And one of them is right outside the payroll office."

"Better talk to the phone company, Kenny."

"I already have. An operator-assisted call was made from that booth at six-ten P.M. to the Diamond Flush bar in Las Vegas, person-to-person. There's no record of who the other person was."

"The Diamond Flush," Gamble repeated. "That ring any bells with you?"

"You're the Vegas authority. Me, I don't know one joint from another. I'm sending a couple of men over to check it out."

"Cancel that. I'm closer than they are."

There was a short silence; Neff was not accustomed to having his orders countermanded. "If that's what you want."

"It is. Another thing I want is for you to arrange a meeting, first thing in the morning, with all other agencies and departments involved in the investigation. I need to know exactly who's doing what, and why."

"Okay, I'll set it up for my office." Neff corrected himself. "I mean your office."

Gamble chuckled. "Just be sure to have your name scraped off the door before I get there." He added, "I'm only kidding, Kenny." But he wasn't sure that Neff believed him.

39

Night had fallen by the time he reached Las Vegas. The gambling capital was doing its best to stave off the darkness. Along the broad thoroughfare called the Strip, towering hotels and squat motels blazed with light. Any one of the huge electric marquees put the rising moon to shame. And if that were not sufficient, the headlamps of countless automobiles hurtled up and down the boulevard in the ceaseless pursuit of the pleasure that always seemed to be somewhere else.

The downtown district to the north—old Las Vegas—was no less gaudy but considerably more tawdry. A tiny handful of the hotels and casinos rivaled their upstart cousins on the Strip. The vast majority courted those who sought entertainment on the cheap. Here there were no lavish buffets and star-studded revues. This was the domain of the one buck breakfast and five buck hooker. The stores remained open until midnight or beyond. From them the sidewalk trade could purchase peekaboo lingerie ("Put New Life in Your Old Wife") and western jackets studded with rhinestones, imported—or deported—liquor at discount prices, prefabricated food guaranteed to produce indigestion and exotic remedies to cure it, and art works best suited to a bordello.

Yet for all its lack of class—or perhaps even because of it —this cut-rate Gomorrah suffered from no shortage of customers. Tourists mostly, they marched the length of Fremont Street and back again, determinedly seeking out the wickedness which, in their own home towns, they would have been the first to condemn.

Few of the economy-class sinners ventured onto the side streets and so the Diamond Flush, whose comparatively modest sign could not even be glimpsed from Fremont, catered for the most part to the city's permanent population. While the cocktail lounge contained the obligatory slot machines, it offered no floor show or other inducements. Its

40

clientele came to drink and to strike up friendships with the opposite sex.

The lone bartender—Steverino, if the name embroidered on his silk shirt was to be believed—and the two cocktail waitresses appeared more than enough to handle the small crowd. "It's always like this about now," Steverino explained. "Three to five, we get the happy hour bunch. Then it falls off through dinnertime and doesn't pick up again until around ten."

"How about last Monday? Or were you on duty?"

"Man, I own the joint—so I'm damn near always on duty." Steverino eyed him narrowly. "You the heat?"

"Do I look like I am?"

"No, you don't have the look exactly. But you sure as hell have the sound. What's the beef?"

"Just a routine investigation. About six o'clock last Monday evening a long distance person-to-person call was made to your number here from Punta Fierro, California. I need to know who that call was for."

"Suppose you tell me why first," Steverino parried.

"You know the rules," Gamble chided. "I ask the questions. You answer them. That way we stay friends."

The mild threat made the bartender chuckle. "Okay, I remember the call. It was for Maggi."

"Maggi who?"

"Maggi Lane, one of my barhops." Gamble looked around sharply at the two waitresses. Steverino shook his head. "Huh-uh. She's not here."

"Any idea what was said?"

"I didn't listen in. I figured it had to be that Fred character, so—"

"Fred Towler?"

Steverino shrugged. "If you say so. All I know is Fred.

41

Anyway, he was the only one who ever phoned her here. They had a thing going, hot and heavy." He added virtuously, "Not that it was any of my business. Maggi did her job and Fred was a damn good customer."

His use of the past tense caused Gamble's eyebrows to shoot up. "Was? That sounds like you don't expect to see him any more."

"He only hung around because of Maggi. Now that she's gone—"

"Gone? Where?"

"Who knows? She just up and quit. These dames drift around all the time. Maggi stayed longer than most. I thought she'd leave a lot sooner than she did. She never really dug the work and she wouldn't butter up the customers for tips, the way a girl has to if she wants to make a decent living. Standoffish, too much a lady, know what I mean? Fred was the only guy I ever saw her give a tumble to. He must have had something the others didn't, at least for her."

Yes, Gamble thought, and that something was ploot. "Exactly when did Maggi quit?"

It was, he learned without surprise, shortly after receiving the long distance telephone call. Steverino had not heard from her since; neither did he have a photograph of his former employee. The best he could furnish was a general description: age late twenties or early thirties, height about five foot four, a Latin look with dark hair and eyes, a "not bad" figure and a face to match . . . and the belief that she resided at the Stafford Arms.

"If Maggi should come back—or if you hear from her— please call me immediately." He wrote down the number of the NRC security office in Los Angeles. "Collect, of course."

"Sure—but I doubt if I'll be seeing her again." Steverino nodded sagely. "I'm betting that Fred finally convinced her to go off with him. He was just dying to take her away from all this."

"That's a good way to put it," Gamble agreed.

The Stafford Arms was within easy walking distance of the Diamond Flush. Maggi Lane had lived there for several months, renting a single room on a week-to-week basis. However, she lived there no longer. She had moved out the previous Monday evening, suddenly and without advance notice, giving some sort of family crisis as her excuse. The Stafford was sorry to see her leave. She had been an ideal tenant, quiet and clean, who paid her bill promptly and created no disturbance.

"These single girls can be a headache," the night manager confided. "They come to Vegas figuring to get work on the Strip—and when that doesn't pan out, they turn to hustling. But Miss Lane wasn't like that. A real lady."

The hotel record listed no forwarding address. The manager guessed that Maggi's destination might be Los Angeles. "She got mail from there sometimes—when she did get mail, that is. I assumed that's where she was from. And since she mentioned that her family needed her in a hurry . . ."

Which might be true—but Gamble reflected that, in these socially troubled times, there were all sorts of families. "How did she leave? By car?"

Yes and no. Maggi didn't own an automobile so the manager had called a cab for her. From the dispatcher, Gamble learned that one of their taxis had picked up a fare at the Stafford Arms a little before midnight the previous Monday. It had discharged its passenger at McCarran Field.

A half-dozen airlines operated out of McCarran on a regular basis. Of these, only three listed outgoing flights between midnight and six A.M. One was bound for Portland, the

43

second for Dallas–Forth Worth via Phoenix. Logic dictated that Maggi Lane had embarked on the third, destination Los Angeles, although her name appeared nowhere on the passenger manifest. However, the airlines required merely that their passengers pay the fare. They did not demand proof of identity.

Neither had Fred Towler, unfortunately for himself. It seemed likely that he had been the hijackers' dupe rather than their accomplice. Infatuated, he had taken Maggi Lane at face value. At her coaxing, no doubt, he had thrown security to the wind ("Hi, baby, guess what? I'm just about to shove off and I'll see you in the morning . . .") and by doing so provided the hijackers with the information they sought. To gain it had been Maggi's only purpose in cultivating him, she who had never given any other customer a tumble. How else to account for her precipitous departure, without waiting to greet her lover—unless she knew he was already as good as dead?

A real lady, quiet and clean; that was what the night manager had termed her. The same description might be applied to a black widow spider.

The
Pitfall

THE INTERNAL SECURITY SECTION of the Nuclear Regulatory Commission, Southwestern Region, was located in the federal office building near the heart of downtown Los Angeles. It was the smallest and, in normal times, the quietest of the governmental agencies headquartered there. But these were not normal times. Now it served as the command post for the massive search operation. As such, it was the home base for nearly one hundred investigators and special experts called in from as far east as Chicago and as far north as Seattle, and space was at a premium.

For that reason, Neff convened the meeting Gamble had requested at a comparatively quiet hour, seven A.M. Although he had come the farthest of all, Gamble was the first to arrive, having driven straight through from Las Vegas to spend what remained of the night on the uncomfortable naugahyde couch in the inner office. The men who assembled to meet him, yawning and glumly clutching cups of coffee, were drawn from the FBI, the Defense Intelligence Agency, the Secret Service and the State Department's Bureau of Intelligence and Research, since counter-terrorist operations had been made a joint responsibility. However, due to the specialized nature of the case, the primary responsibility for pursuing it rested on Nerk, now embodied in the person of Gus Gamble. Inter-service rivalry being what it was, he suspected that his first task was to convince the others that he merited their confidence.

The task was made more difficult by the fact that he knew none of them. There was a time when he would have been intimately acquainted with each. But that time was long past and strangers had replaced his former associates. A few knew him by reputation; most, however, had never heard of him. And so they regarded him, if not with suspicion, at least with a certain reserve.

He met the challenge head-on. "You're probably wondering who I am and what I'm doing here. Good questions. One answer is that, once upon a time, I was the leading expert on atomic security. If you want my credentials, try this: I predicted the hijacking years ago. Of course, there's nothing more tiresome than yesterday's expert." He smiled. "So I guess a better answer might be that I'm the world's worst loser. When I play, I play to win. Close is only good enough with horseshoes and hand grenades. I didn't take this job to preside over a disaster. I don't believe there has to be a disaster. Between us, we've got enough brains and experience and know-how to prevent it—if we use them to the fullest. I promise to use mine. I expect no less from the rest of you."

They had all heard too many pep talks to be easily impressed. Donald Peterson, the man from the State Department's BIR, replied smoothly, "I'm sure that you can count on a maximum effort from everyone."

"Let's define maximum. In my vocabulary, it means a lot

more than merely following established routines and procedures. Anyone can do that. I expect you to begin where the book leaves off. To use your imagination, to be willing to try anything and everything. To turn over every stone, no matter how unpromising it looks—and when you've run out of stones, to go out and find more."

"Subject to your approval, of course."

"As long as you follow my game plan, you can consider that you have my approval."

"Are you saying that you won't require us to clear everything with you?" The cautious request for clarification came from Roy McElwaine, the FBI's special agent-in-charge.

"You're all big boys. There's no reason you should have to ask my permission every time you want to go to the bathroom. Run your own show. All I require is that we keep in touch to avoid unnecessary duplication. Let's have no secrets from each other. This is a team effort"—he refrained from glancing at Neff—"and we're not out to score brownie points. As long as we win, it doesn't matter a damn who gets the credit."

He had finally impressed them; a commander who did not insist on gathering all power into his own hands was a refreshing novelty. They sat up a bit more confidently and their expressions mirrored a respect previously lacking. That hurdle behind him, Gamble said briskly, "Okay, let's see where we stand. I assume we all understand the problem. The ploot's been missing for a little over a week now. That means that, under optimum conditions, the hijackers could have their bomb in another week."

"Are we absolutely sure that they intend to build a bomb?" asked George Upshaw. He was the Secret Service representative. "Could they have heisted the ploot for resale elsewhere?"

"Possible but unlikely. There's no ready market for it. In

any case, whether the hijackers are middlemen or the ultimate consumer, the ploot is almost certain to wind up in bomb form, sooner or later. So our problem is the same."

Colonel Sid Mulkey, who as the DIA liaison spoke for the military intelligence establishment, raised a hand. "Suppose it turns out that they don't have the skill or the know-how to build the bomb?"

"They had the skill and the know-how to break into a truck that supposedly couldn't be broken into," Gamble reminded him. "Anyway, as long as they've got the ploot, they can use the threat to blackmail us. Which might serve their purpose nearly as well."

Mulkey grimaced. "It would certainly help if we knew what their purpose was, wouldn't it?"

"Money. Power. Perhaps both."

"I suggest there may well be Communist involvement," Neff put in.

His cherished theory won no supporters. McElwaine said what Gamble preferred not to. "This isn't the Soviets' bag. I'm willing to credit them with just about anything except stupidity—and for them to pull something like this would be the ultimate in stupidity. The hijacking was a terrorist operation, pure and simple. Let's not waste our time chasing bogeymen."

Neff subsided with a scowl. Gamble said, "Expand on that, Mac. What sort of terrorists? Foreign or domestic?"

Domestic, in McElwaine's view. The federal government maintained a computerized filing system—called Octopus— which contained the names of every known terrorist in every country throughout the world and also kept an up-to-date record of their movements for the purpose of predicting their actions. Octopus had not anticipated the hijacking nor had subsequent studies of the files produced anything of value. The Irish Republican Army and the Palestinian guerrillas, who were responsible for the bulk of international terrorist activities, appeared to be innocent in this case.

Consequently, the FBI was digging into the domestic subversive groups. McElwaine enumerated them; the list covered a broad spectrum, from far left to far right. "New World Liberation Front, Black Liberation Army, Red Guerrilla Family, Secret Army Organization, Weather Underground, Emiliano Zapata Unit . . . They all have the capability but we haven't been able to pin the tail on any one of those donkeys."

"Could be we're dealing with virgins," Upshaw observed. "If so, that makes it even tougher. I'll take the professional every time. They at least give you a handle to grab."

"I think we've got our handle," Gamble said. They listened attentively as he recounted his investigation of the Diamond Flush and the conclusions to be drawn from it. "So now we know how the ambush was arranged. The hijackers used the oldest trick in the book—sex—to get the information they needed. But to do it, they had to put one of their people on display. Maggi Lane is undoubtedly an alias but she may have used it before. And we can cross-check with age, physical description and m.o."

"Since Maggi apparently headed for Los Angeles," Upshaw said, "wouldn't it be wise to ask the L.A. police to look for her?"

"I don't think we can, George. We can't give the locals a piece of the story without giving them more than we want them to know at this point. Our own people, they'll keep their mouths shut. But we don't have any rein on outsiders."

"I suppose you're right," Upshaw agreed reluctantly. "But if I were one of them, if this was my home town, I wouldn't appreciate not being told it might blow up at any minute."

"The answer to that is that we don't have any reason to believe that L.A. is the intended target. Maybe it is, maybe it isn't—but until we've more to go on, there's really no reason to warn Los Angeles in preference, say, to Oshkosh or Tallahassee."

This provoked speculation on what the intended target might be. The guesses ranged from Hoover Dam and the San Francisco Bay bridges to Manhattan and the U.S. Capitol. Gamble terminated the discussion. "We've got more pertinent questions to answer. For example, the hijackers used an antitank cannon, or a recoilless rifle, to stop the truck. That sort of weapon isn't easy to come by. So where did they get it? Colonel?"

Mulkey shrugged. "Our own military stockpiles are the most likely source. The latest study shows that, over the past five years, we've lost more than seven thousand weapons of various types. We suspect that most of them wound up in the hands of various terrorist groups, both here and overseas."

"Anything as large as the cannon the hijackers used?"

"Quite probably. I recall one batch that was taken down in Georgia which included a sixty millimeter cannon, a bazooka, mortars and machine guns. We recovered most of that. I'll ask each service for an inventory on what we haven't recovered."

"Include high explosives, chemical and plastic. If we can find out where the hijackers got their arms, it might give us another handle to grab. Along the same line, I have here a list of the materials Dr. Sorbo believes would be required to build the bomb. I'm sorry to say that they can be purchased at any good-sized hardware store. So that means we're going to have to check every good-sized hardware store in the Los Angeles area."

"Why just L.A.?" McElwaine inquired wryly. "What about Oshkosh and Tallahassee?"

"I figure that they'd want to build their bomb as close as possible to where they stole the ploot. A big city's the best place to hide—and L.A. is the closest big city. Besides, Maggi Lane came here. Of course, I could be mistaken."

Donald Peterson regarded him slyly. "The way it was told to me, you're never mistaken."

"There's a first time for everything. Okay, that's about it as far as I'm concerned. Mac, lean harder on your informers. You may have to burn a few, but there'll never be a better reason. Colonel, get us that inventory. The rest of you, start turning over stones. Any questions?"

"Yeah," said Upshaw as they got to their feet. "There's the damnedest rumor going around . . . Is it true that you're also a Jesuit priest?"

One or two laughed, then looked startled at Gamble's nod. "Don't let it shake you up," he told them. "If you can get me the confessions of the people who stole our ploot, I won't ask for yours."

"That was quite a pep talk," Neff remarked when they were alone. "Reminded me of my old football coach. The team that won't be beaten can't be beaten. The game's never over till the final whistle. They put on their pants one leg at a time, men, just like you. Et cetera, et cetera."

"What position did you play, Kenny?"

"Quarterback."

"I should have guessed. You're not used to blocking." He gave Neff the sheaf of registration cards from the Desert Sands Resort. "Have someone start checking out these names. I think one of them may be a phony. And not necessarily John Smith, either."

"Another hunch?"

"They made me what I am." He grinned. "Write your own punch line, Kenny."

An interim report was on his desk before noon. Of the nineteen possibilities, twelve had been located easily by tele-

51

phone and were apparently genuine. Six of the remaining seven either had no telephone or had not answered it. The seventh name caused Gamble to discard the rest. David Johnson—a name even more common than Smith—had listed a nonexistent address on a nonexistent street.

It was not the dead end it first appeared to be. Johnson had been required to furnish the Desert Sands with the license number of his vehicle, a Dodge pickup with camper conversion, suitable for sleeping six. While the license might be fictitious also, Gamble queried the Department of Motor Vehicles in Sacramento and was rewarded with the information that the plates had been issued to a David A. and Myra L. Jeffords, 3460 Diversion Drive, Los Angeles.

"David Johnson, David Jeffords," Gamble mused. "Same first name, same last initial. Interesting what?"

"Why would anyone register under a false name and still give his correct license number?" Neff wondered. "Doesn't make sense."

"A man tells me his name is Johnson and I'll accept that. But if he drives up in a Dodge with one license and tells me it's a Ford with another license, that might make me a wee bit suspicious. And suspicious is what the hijackers didn't want to make anyone. Let's see what we can find out about Mr. Jeffords."

The information was easily come by. In a society increasingly dominated by the computer, a citizen could not work for wages or operate a business, maintain a bank account, acquire a credit card or a driver's license—or even borrow a book from the library—without finding himself tucked away in at least one memory bank, and usually several. David A. Jeffords was no exception. Gamble learned that he was forty-one years old, white, five foot seven inches in height and a hundred and forty-five pounds in weight. He and his wife were childless; they were buying their home. A structural engineer, Jeffords had been employed locally by the Sumner-Moulton Company, which manufactured polyvinyl chloride; significantly, it had supplied some of the material used in the construction of the second nuclear reactor at Punta Fierro. Six months earlier, a decline in the firm's fortunes had caused Jeffords to be terminated. Since then, he had been living off unemployment benefits and his savings; both were nearly exhausted.

Gamble found the picture intriguing. "An engineer with some connection to Punta Fierro, out of work and running out of dough while the bills keep rolling in . . . That's an awful feeling. It could make a man desperate."

"Desperate enough for murder and hijacking?" Neff said dubiously. "Hell, Jeffords doesn't even have a speeding ticket. Not exactly the criminal type."

"Maybe he has friends who are. And maybe, if we ask him real nice, he'll introduce us."

Diversion Drive was a short and winding street tucked into a small canyon on the fringe of Griffith Park. The park, flung like a shapeless blanket across the eastern flank of the Santa Monica mountains, was Los Angeles' principal gift to those who coveted open space within the city limits. Its broad and often precipitous acreage contained a zoo, a planetarium, a golf course and an outdoor theater, plus trails for horses and meadows for picnickers. The residential neighborhoods which surrounded it had once been considered exclusive. These days realtors called them choice or, in some cases, merely convenient, tacitly acknowledging that the very rich had long since moved on to Bel Air and Brentwood, leaving their pseudo-castles and mini-mansions to the middle class.

The sycamores and laurels which lined Diversion Drive had been planted by the original subdividers. Saplings then, they now reared as high as the tallest house and their branches met above the pavement to create the impression of a forest glade rather than a city street. It seemed a most unlikely hideout for a gang of ruthless hijackers—but Gamble reflected that it might have been chosen for exactly that reason.

He drove to the end of the quiet lane and back again. At this hour, four o'clock on a chilly afternoon, most of the residents were either absent or indoors. In one yard, an elderly man was trimming his Eugenia hedge with electric shears. In another, a pair of teen-agers were tossing a frisbie back and forth. Otherwise, Diversion Drive was devoid of life.

Gamble was careful not to pay more attention to 3460 than to the others. The middle-aged house, two stories of white stucco and red tile and wrought iron grillwork, was similar to many of its neighbors and scarcely worthy of a second glance. One glance was sufficient, anyway. The nearly new Dodge camper van parked in the driveway demonstrated that this was the Jeffords' residence.

He turned the corner and stopped behind the unmarked sedan which contained the members of his strike force. Neff had assembled a group of blooded veterans, men trained in search-and-seizure tactics. A back-up unit, several times larger, waited within easy calling distance.

Gamble gathered his team around him. "Third house from the corner on the left. I didn't see anyone, but the camper's in the drive so I figure that our bird is in the nest."

"How do you want to handle it?" Neff asked.

"I'd rather not give them any more advance notice than we have to." He saw that suited the rest; those who had not viewed the gutted armored truck had heard about it. If the weapon which had produced that carnage was in the house, no one wished to afford the hijackers another opportunity to

54

employ it. "What say we red-dog it?"

"Okay. Who wants the honor of opening up the hole?"

"It's my party," Gamble said. "I'll take the point."

"You've got it." Neff turned to the others. "Caldwell, you circle around to the back and make sure they don't duck out on us. Let us know when you're in position. Perry, you and I'll handle the pass rush. Martinez, you cover."

He began to pass out ordnance and equipment, carbines and gas grenades and walkie-talkies. "That should do for openers. We'll save the heavy stuff for if and when." He regarded Gamble questioningly. "How about you? Want a pistol?"

Gamble drew out the crucifix he wore on a chain around his throat. "I'll stick with this."

"Okay," Neff agreed with a tight smile. "We'll handle the shooting. You handle the praying. Caldwell, on your horse."

Caldwell darted off, disappearing between the houses. The rest waited silently, stamping their feet or rocking back and forth on their heels to relieve the mounting tension. Martinez, the burly Chicano, asked Gamble shyly, "That for real —about you being a priest?"

"Yes. Are you Catholic?"

"Not a very good one." Martinez knelt clumsily, hampered by the armament he carried. "Would you give me your blessing, Father?"

Gamble heard Neff's stifled snort of derision. He ignored it. Placing his hand on Martinez's helmeted head, he began, "Most gracious heavenly Father, I beseech you—"

Caldwell's voice on the walkie-talkie interrupted him. "Red Dog One to Red Dog Leader. In position and ready for love."

Gamble completed the blessing swiftly. Neff said, "Well, if the service is over, let's get secular."

He led the way at a rapid trot, Perry following and Gamble

55

bringing up the rear. They rounded the corner onto Diversion Drive, cutting across the lawns and staying close to the houses in order to render their approach inconspicuous. Martinez, in the unmarked sedan, paralleled their path.

As they reached the house adjacent to their objective, its front door opened. A woman stepped out to retrieve the evening newspaper. Her eyes widened as they took in the armed men, and her mouth fell open with surprise.

"Federal agents!" Neff warned in a low harsh voice. "Get inside, lady, and stay away from the windows!"

The woman skittered back into her home; the door slammed behind her. Gamble could hear her calling frantically to her children. If he could hear her, so too could the occupants of the Jeffords house. However, a mother screaming at her kids wasn't likely to arouse their suspicions. In any case, it was too late to worry about it.

Twisted juniper grew tall on either side of the Jeffords' porch, like twin sentinels. Neff and Perry crouched in their concealment; Gamble joined them. At curbside, Martinez was out of the sedan and was sprawled across its hood, his rifle at the ready. Neff used the walkie-talkie to inform Caldwell, in a voice barely above a whisper, that the attack was about to begin. He nodded at Gamble. "You're on."

Gamble mounted the steps to the porch. He rang the bell and listened to the far-off chiming. There was no immediate response; he rang the bell again. Then he heard another sound, footsteps approaching down an uncarpeted hallway. The door swung open. A man's pudgy face peered out, eyes blinking in the sunlight.

"David Jeffords?" Gamble asked huskily.

"That's right," the man acknowledged. "What can I do for you?"

His question went unanswered. The opening of the door, like the snap of a football, had sent the Nerk team into action. Neff and Perry nearly bowled Gamble over as they charged past him into the house.

"Collar him!" Neff snapped. A stiff-arm in passing sent Jeffords reeling back against the wall. "We'll take the rest." He raced down the long hallway. Perry bounded up the stairs to the second floor.

David Jeffords, stunned by the swift and unexpected invasion of his home, cried out, "Hey, you can't—" He stopped his protest abruptly, cringing in terror. "For God's sake, don't shoot me!"

Martinez had arrived to join the battle. Armed with both carbine and pistol, dark eyes flashing and mustache bristling beneath his helmet, he resembled a space age version of a Mexican bandido. Roughly, he spun Jeffords around. "Both hands on the wall, feet apart."

"Don't kill me," Jeffords begged. "You can have anything you want, just don't—"

"Shut up." Martinez ran a hand over his captive's body to assure himself that he was unarmed. "On the floor, mister—face down."

Jeffords obeyed with alacrity; there was no fight in him. Standing over the prostrate man, Gamble and Martinez listened tensely for the expected commotion in another part of the house. It did not come. All they heard was the rasp of their own breath and the whimpering of their prisoner. "Maybe I'd better go after them," Martinez muttered.

It wasn't necessary. Both Neff and Perry reappeared almost simultaneously. Perry came down the stairs empty-handed. Neff had been more fortunate. He had a second captive by the arm. This one was female and, for just an instant, Gamble dared to hope that it was Maggi Lane. But only for an instant; there was little similarity besides gender between Towler's treacherous sweetheart and this middle-aged woman whose body was engulfed in a tentlike muu-

57

muu. The gown's vivid colors emphasized the stark pallor of a face that once possibly had been pretty and was now bloated with fat.

"Nobody here but this chicken," Neff reported. "Claims she's Mrs. Jeffords."

Her frightened eyes caught sight of the man lying on the floor. Her voice rose in a scream. "David! Oh, my God, what have you done to him?"

"We haven't done anything to him," Gamble told her, in a tone which made "not yet" implicit. He nudged Jeffords with his toe. "You can get up now. We've got a few questions to ask you. Where are the rest of your friends hiding?"

The pair stared at him mutely. Gamble repeated the question. The woman found her voice first. "We don't know what you're talking about, Officer," she quavered.

"Officer?" her husband echoed, as if the possibility had never occurred to him that the intruders were lawmen. Now that it had, his face registered both relief and indignation. "You mean you're cops?"

Neff held up his identification. "Federal agents."

"Federal . . . Say, what's this all about, anyway?"

"Are you David A. Jeffords?" Gamble interrupted. "Is that your camper in the driveway?"

"Yeah, I'm Jeffords and that's my camper, but—"

"Were you registered at the Desert Sands Resort in Barstow ten days ago under the name of David Johnson?"

Jeffords hesitated. His wife did not. "Of course he wasn't! You've made some kind of terrible mistake, Officer. David's never been near Barstow. And certainly not ten days ago. He was in San José for a job interview."

"Good. He'll have a chance to prove it. Jeffords, you're under arrest. Kenny, read him his rights."

"You can't do that!" Mrs. Jeffords protested. "David hasn't done anything. Tell them, honey. Tell them we'll sue

58

them if they don't leave you alone."

Jeffords licked his lips. "As a matter of fact," he said in a nearly inaudible voice, "I was in Barstow."

She stared at him, astonished. "You were? What on earth for?"

He couldn't meet her eyes. "Well, you see, the job interview didn't pan out. You weren't expecting me home till Tuesday, so I thought I'd grab a couple days' rest before getting back to pounding the pavement—"

"But why didn't you let me know? I could have met you ...." Her voice trailed off and her face congealed in cold suspicion. "The Desert Sands Resort in Barstow," she said as if pronouncing sentence. "Isn't that the same place where Sonia was staying?"

"Sonia?" Gamble asked with a sudden clammy intuition. "That wouldn't be Mrs. Sonia Wick, would it?"

"Yes, it certainly would. She's my best friend—at least, I thought she was." She tried to smile; the effect was ghastly.

Jeffords wore the look of a trapped animal. "Myra, don't go jumping to conclusions. It's not the way it sounds. I just happened to bump into Sonia up there. I was going to tell you about it—"

"Please don't bother." She drew back from his imploring grasp, her betrayal made even more painful by the fact that it had been revealed in the presence of strangers. The glance she gave Gamble was nearly as venomous as the one she gave her betrayer. "Is there anything more, Officer?"

Gamble shook his head. Myra Jeffords gathered the muumuu about her ample figure like a toga and, with it, what little pride remained. She stalked off down the hall, outrage evident in every step. Her husband trotted after her, pleading, without even bothering to ask permission, made oblivious by the domestic catastrophe to all else. A door slammed behind them.

59

There was a moment of silence. Neff broke it to supply a sardonic epitaph to the fiasco. "You forgot to give them your blessing, Father."

"Seems I've led you on a wild-goose chase," Gamble admitted. He had come here hoping to apprehend a hijacker. He had merely unmasked an adulterer. "Sorry, gentlemen."

Neff wasn't willing to let him off the hook so easily. "Well, it hasn't been a total loss. You didn't catch the hijackers— but you sure as hell did a number on a marriage." His smile, like his tone, was a masterpiece of sarcasm. "It's good to know that you haven't lost your touch."

The blunder, while embarrassing, was by no means fatal. It even had its comic side—although it was doubtful that the Jeffords would find much to amuse them. For that matter, neither did Gamble. More than his pride was involved. To be effective, he needed to have the confidence of the forces he commanded. Men respond to strong leadership, are inspired by it to give their best. Once they suspect it to be weak, they become dispirited and, potentially as disastrous, are tempted to take the leadership into their own hands.

It was equally important that he not lose confidence in himself. Yesterday, when his hunches seemed to be paying off with their former regularity, he had decided that nothing had really changed, that he was still as good as he had ever been. The match folder clue, which he had optimistically counted on to bring the case to a speedy conclusion, had come to naught. Anyone could make a mistake, of course, but Gamble—who prided himself on his intuition and who, in fact, had built his reputation on it—couldn't help but wonder if the years had taken their toll, after all.

He forced the doubt aside. Don't panic, he told himself; you haven't lost a thing. Nevertheless, he was anxious to demonstrate it, not only to the world but to himself.

The opportunity was not long in coming. Roy McElwaine telephoned late Thursday afternoon to report jubilantly that the FBI had located Maggi Lane. Where? "Look out your window, Gus. She's practically within spitting distance."

Gamble stared at the building across the street, a glassy tower which housed the Los Angeles County Jail. "Don't tell me she's in the slammer."

"Yep. And has been for better than a week. She flew in from Vegas just like you figured. One of the local narcs happened to be working the Burbank airport. Maggi has a record as a drug offender. He shook her down on general principles and, sure enough, she had a purseful of pot."

"What's her status?"

"She was arraigned last Wednesday. Bail was set but not posted. Her case comes up first thing in the morning."

"Who's representing her?"

"Public defender. If you were to judge by appearances, Maggi doesn't have a friend in the world. Except that we know better." McElwaine chuckled. "By the way, Maggi Lane isn't her real name, again like you figured. Try Magdalena Lopez."

"How did you make the connection?"

"She had an ID in the Maggi Lane name on her when she was booked. L.A.'s computer told my computer . . . and my computer told me."

"What else did your computer tell you?"

"Born Magdalena Huerta, native of Puerto Rico. Married to a Eugenio Lopez, a no goodnick who was mixed up in radical politics on the island. He's deceased now. Maggi— Magdalena—doesn't appear to have been political herself. Her allegiance is to the almighty dollar. When Lopez's money ran out, she ran out too and moved up to New York. Did a little acting, a little modeling, then found true happiness as a call girl. Last year she drifted out here, got herself busted and did ninety days." McElwaine paused. "Further the computer sayeth not."

Gamble pursed his lips thoughtfully. "Remind me to send it flowers. We've gotten our first real break, Mac. Now we have to see what we can do with it."

Neff, at least, did not feel that this presented a problem. "We could have blown days looking for her," he gloated. "And here she is right on our doorstep, gift-wrapped. The only thing I can't figure is why her friends didn't bail her out a week ago."

"They don't know that we've connected her with Towler or that we know that Maggi Lane and Magdalena Lopez are one and the same. Maybe they figure that jail is the safest place for her right now, rather than running around loose where she could get into trouble. And so they told her to cool it, to take her jolt and they'll get back to her later."

"That's their big mistake, then. She's going to sing like a bird."

Gamble shook his head. "I don't want her interrogated."

Neff gaped at him. "Why the hell not?"

"To begin with, we don't have a case against her. So far it's all conjecture. We can't prove that Towler furnished her with the information on 319 or—even if he did—that she passed it along to the others."

"We can prove she got his phone call—"

"Can we? Okay, let's say that we can. Can we prove what was said? Only two people know for sure. One of them is dead and the other isn't going to tell us. She'll claim he just called to say how much he missed her—or to ask her to marry him—or something equally innocent."

"Then why did she cut out in such a hurry?"

"Don't you suppose she's ready for that question? 'Oh, Fred was getting too serious and I didn't really want to marry him and so I thought it would be better for both of us . . . Ploot? What's that? A hijacking? Never heard of it.' "

"I can sweat the truth out of her," Neff vowed.

"For a young man, you've got some pretty old-fashioned ideas. The bright lights and rubber hose are long gone. You start muscling her and Maggi's going to demand an attorney. That's her constitutional right—that, and the right to remain silent—and I'm sure she's well up on them. She has to be a pretty cool customer to have played the part she did. She's been down the interrogation road before. We're not going to frighten her into admitting that she's an accomplice to murder, not unless we can back it up with solid evidence. And we can't."

"We could offer her a deal. Her neck for theirs."

"That works only when the criminal is convinced that there's no other way out. How are you going to convince Maggi of that with the evidence we have? She'll sit there and laugh at you, Kenny. Even worse, she'll manage somehow to get word to the rest of the gang . . . and we'll be no better off than when we started."

"We've got her and I say we should sweat her. Sure, there's a risk involved—but it's a hell of a lot better than doing nothing."

"I don't propose that we should do nothing. I do propose that we employ another method to get the information we want, one which doesn't involve letting Maggi know that we're getting it."

"What do you suggest—prayer?" Neff could not conceal his sneer.

"That's always the best way to begin," Gamble replied mildly. "Provided that you follow it up with action."

"Wait a minute!" Neff exclaimed. "I've got an idea where we can have it both ways, yours and mine. Maggi's Catholic, right? She must have a lot on her conscience. So suppose that a priest shows up at the jail tonight to hear confessions—and just suppose that this priest's name is Gamble . . ." He sat back, delighted at his ingenuity.

"That's out of the question."

"Why? It fits your specifications, doesn't it? She'll tell us what we're after and never know she's told us."

"I can't profane my office, Kenny. You should understand that."

"I don't understand that and I don't understand you," Neff replied heatedly. "Exactly where do you stand in this, anyway? Are you a cop or are you a priest? I'd like to know."

"I'm trying to be both. As a cop, I'll do everything I can to make Maggi Lane give us the information we need. But as a priest, I cannot and will not violate the sanctity of the confessional."

"Even if that means we don't get the information?"

"Yes—if that should be the choice. Luckily, it isn't. There's another way to achieve the same result."

"Well, if you won't interrogate her and you won't trick her . . ." Neff shook his head. "Damned if I see what other option is open to us."

"It ought to be fairly obvious," Gamble said. "We turn her loose."

The proposal produced an explosion as Gamble suspected it might, composed of equal parts astonishment and indignation with a generous dash of ridicule thrown in. He let Neff get it out of his system. When the younger man finally ran out of words to express his violent opposition, Gamble asked, straight-faced, "Are you trying to tell me that you don't think much of my idea?"

Neff realized that he was being kidded but was too perturbed to reply in kind. He said stiffly, "I consider it so asinine that I can't believe you're serious."

"I've already explained why I believe that interrogating

Maggi would be nonproductive. As for your second suggestion, we could play a modified version by planting a policewoman in her cell. She might be able to win Maggi's confidence to the point where she'd spill her guts. But I'd say the odds are no better than ten to one. And, even if we win, it would take time, and time is what we don't have much of. With me so far?" Neff shrugged, a gesture which expressed neither agreement nor disagreement. "Okay, Maggi is due to be tried in the morning. We arrange with the district attorney to have the charges against her dismissed. It shouldn't take too much persuasion. The case is likely to be thrown out anyway. The public defender will probably be able to demonstrate that the evidence against her was obtained illegally."

"We can find something to hold her on," Neff said stubbornly.

"No doubt. But let's say that Maggi walks out of the courthouse tomorrow free as a bird. And without any worry that we've connected her to the hijacking. What will she normally do next? She'll go to wherever it was she was headed when she was arrested. Dollars to doughnuts, that's to join her friends. And when she does, we'll be right behind her."

"Sure," Neff agreed. "We follow Maggi, she leads us to the rest of the gang, we grab them and the ploot—and it's all over."

"I'm glad you see it my way, Kenny."

"Like hell! Oh, it sounds easy, sitting here talking about it. But it's as risky as walking a tightrope across Niagara Falls. Suppose she manages to lose the tail?"

"There's an element of risk in everything. In this case, I believe it's an acceptable risk." He saw that Neff remained unconvinced and he sighed. "Trust me, Kenny. I know what I'm doing."

"Like with Jeffords?"

Gamble kept his temper. "Like with Towler being the security leak. I'm one out of two. How are you doing?"

"I haven't had my turn at bat yet," Neff reminded him curtly. "Okay, it's your decision. But I want to go on record as disapproving it. I'll even put it in writing." He smiled thinly as though to demonstrate that he too had a sense of humor. "So that you'll have the pleasure of watching me eat my words if I'm wrong."

Gamble smiled also. "Bon appétit."

Gamble was in superior court the next morning when the case against Maggi Lane was dismissed, on motion by the district attorney, for lack of evidence. From an unobtrusive seat in the rear, he studied the woman who had played Delilah to Fred Towler's Samson. As is so often the case, it was difficult for the dispassionate observer to imagine what her fatal fascination had amounted to. Maggi was by no means a raving beauty. She did possess a certain sultry attractiveness but without the smoldering sexuality to give it life. While her lips were full and sensual, the dark eyes were coldly calculating; Maggi appeared to be more ice than fire. Yet Towler had apparently not found her so. It only went to demonstrate the power a determined woman—almost any woman, for that matter—could wield against a vulnerable man when it suited her purpose.

Maggi accepted the dismissal of the charge against her with more bewilderment than delight. Freed, she slipped out of the courtroom and returned to the jail to retrieve her suitcase, the contents of which had been carefully (and fruitlessly) examined. During the night one of the two locks had been replaced. It now concealed a tiny radio transmitter whose steady signal would permit the location of the suitcase —and, presumably, its owner—to be constantly monitored.

66

Gamble was loitering on the steps of the jail when Maggi emerged fifteen minutes later, suitcase in hand. He expected she might hail a cab or board the bus. Instead, she crossed the street and entered the busy drugstore on the corner, trailed at a discreet distance by Martinez.

Gamble joined Neff in the unmarked sedan, one of four, which waited to take up the chase. "What's she up to?" Neff asked tensely.

"Making a phone call. Probably to tell her friends she's out of the joint."

"Think somebody will be coming to pick her up?"

"Maybe. Or maybe they'll tell her to take a cab. Either way, our move's the same."

They waited in silence. At last, Maggi came out of the drugstore, hesitated, then turned back again. She nearly collided with Martinez, who was just emerging. "Oh-oh!" Gamble murmured. "Play it cool, amigo."

Martinez did. He gave the woman a scowl and walked off with a glance at his wristwatch, as if late for an appointment elsewhere. Maggi watched him go.

"She's made him," Neff groaned.

"Don't give up the ship, Kenny. I think she's just being careful. On orders from above, no doubt."

Maggi strolled away in the opposite direction, pausing frequently to glance around with seeming casualness. Finally reassured, she quickened her steps and headed for the taxi stand in the middle of the next block. An empty cab waited there, its driver perched on one fender reading a newspaper. Maggi spoke with him. The driver folded his newspaper and assisted her to enter.

"Looks like we're in business." Gamble picked up the microphone. "Attention, all units. Suspect has just entered a Yellow Cab, number 202, license E77137. It's heading south on Spring Street and we are pursuing. Car Two, fall in behind and prepare to leapfrog. Cars Three and Four, take the parallels."

Neff rapidly closed the gap between the two vehicles to the point where they could keep their quarry in view without making their own presence obvious. The ever-present glut of traffic made concealment easy but pursuit hazardous. The cabbie piloted his vehicle with typical élan, forcing Neff to match his reckless abandon or give up the chase.

Gamble picked up the microphone again. "Vehicle is entering the Harbor Freeway, heading south. All units follow. Helicopter, do you read me?"

"Loud and clear."

"We'll tailgate until you've got a fix on the taxi, then drop back and let Car Two take over. Acknowledge."

"Gotcha," the helicopter pilot responded briefly. A few moments later, he reported that the cab had been identified. Neff slowed down and allowed the second pursuit car to fall in behind the speeding taxi. All four cars continued to rotate their position at regular intervals as the chase continued— so that Maggi Lane, should she glance out the rear window, would see only the normal shifting pattern of traffic behind her.

As they approached each exit, Gamble tensed, expecting that this must surely be the point at which the taxi would depart the freeway. And each time he was mistaken. The strange caravan continued its swift and steady pace until, at last, he could see the tall hotels of Long Beach silhouetted against the sky and, beyond them, the glistening blue waters of the Pacific.

"She gonna visit the *Queen Mary?*" Neff wondered, referring to the former British luxury liner, now the port city's principal tourist attraction.

"The *Mary*'s not the only boat in the harbor. I can think

of worse hiding places."

However, a ship large or small was not Maggi Lane's destination. Her taxi finally swung off the freeway and headed west into the Wilmington district. It was part of the port of Los Angeles, a grimy and unprepossessing waterfront community given over mainly to manufacturing plants, warehouses and fuel storage tanks. There were also a smaller number of retail establishments, shabby for the most part, designed to serve the needs of those who worked here. The taxi stopped at one of these, a small three-story hotel whose name—Pacific Paradise—was its most attractive feature. Maggi paid off the driver and went inside, carrying her suitcase.

Gamble used the radio to marshal his forces. A stakeout was quickly established on all the hotel's exits. One of the chase cars, a van equipped with a concealed camera, was stationed directly across the street from the front door to film all who entered or left the Pacific Paradise. The helicopter was dispatched to the nearby Long Beach airport to stand by should it be needed.

Neff, following a lengthy reconnaissance, reported that Maggi Lane had registered and had been given Room 37, third floor front. "I used the old building inspector cover so I could nose around. She's there, all right. Corner window on the left, that's her."

Gamble eyed the curtain glass thoughtfully. "Well, it's too high for her to jump and the fire escape's on the other side. Is there a telephone in her room?"

"Dumps like that don't have room phones. But there is a pay phone in the hall. I got the number."

"Better see about putting a tap on it, Kenny. And bring back some coffee. We may be here for quite a spell."

In this he was proven correct. The balance of the morning dragged by, its earlier excitement seemingly spent. The Pa-

69

cific Paradise attracted few visitors. Now and then, one of its residents, all of them women, would emerge on some brief errand from which she returned shortly. A laundry truck delivered fresh linen and towels and a trash truck appeared to haul away the week's accumulated refuse. All were photographed, logged and in some cases followed. Otherwise, there was little to relieve the tedium.

Shortly after midday, however, traffic in and out of the hotel picked up appreciably. Earlier, it had been exclusively female; now it was almost entirely male.

"Thought so," Neff grunted. "The joint's a cat house. Guys off the docks and out of the factories, grabbing a nooner. Funny Maggi'd pick a place like that to hole up."

"It's as good a hole as any. And I don't imagine she intends to stay long."

"Well, I wish she'd get a move on. Sitting out here, I'm beginning to feel like a goddam voyeur."

Gamble shared his impatience, but his previous training, both as a lawman and as a priest, equipped him to bear it better. He had hoped that Maggi might lead him directly to the hijackers' lair. Obviously, she had not. But there was every reason to believe that she still would and, given this expectation, he was content to wait her out.

Business at the Pacific Paradise ebbed and flowed throughout the remainder of the day, falling off during the afternoon, picking up again as evening approached. Although Maggi was presumably not involved in it, she did not leave the hotel —or, as far as they were able to determine, her room. Neither did she place nor receive any telephone calls. The vigil continued.

The coming of night was heralded in customary March fashion by the fog which surged in from the ocean, shrouding the land like a clammy blanket. For a short while, the sun strove against it, then, surrendering, vanished and only the

70

rapid deepening of the gloom, gray turning into black, marked the ending of the day. Along the avenue, neon signs flickered on, pallid beacons in the murky night. Lights commenced to glow in the windows of the Pacific Paradise.

Neff, who had been dozing, roused himself with a yawn. "Guess I'd better call in the night shift to relieve us."

"Not just yet. We should be seeing a little action before long. Maggi hasn't had anything to eat since breakfast. She must be getting mighty hungry."

"She's not the only one." But he offered no serious objection to remaining. After enduring the lengthy stakeout, now over eight hours old, he was as eager as Gamble to be present at its conclusion.

Another hour marched slowly by on leaden feet, and still Maggi Lane had not appeared. For the first time, Gamble began to experience uneasiness, a nagging sense that something had gone wrong. He argued it away by crediting it to tension. Maggi was operating on her own timetable, not his, and there was no reason to believe . . . He craned his neck in order to study the third-floor window, as he had done periodically all day. "You sure that's her room?" he asked Neff sharply. "The one on the corner?"

"Damn right, I'm sure."

"It's dark. Every other window on the floor is lighted— and hers isn't."

Neff hastily verified his observation. "She could be taking a long nap." But he didn't sound as though he believed it.

Neither did Gamble. He grabbed the microphone. "Gamble to all units. Neff and I are going in for a look around. Somebody peel off and cover the front."

They crossed the silent street and entered the equally silent lobby. The clerk didn't even look up from his newspaper; the appearance of two male visitors was nothing out of the ordinary.

71

The Pacific Paradise boasted no elevator; they climbed the stairs. The third-floor hallway was badly lighted and its uncarpeted floor in need of a broom. The air smelled as old as the grimy walls which held it prisoner. In one of the rooms a radio was playing loudly. Some of the doors stood ajar, not for ventilation but as an indication that the occupants were open for business. The door to Room 37, however, was closed.

Neff knocked on it. "Open up, Debbie!" he called loudly. "It's Big Daddy, and he's brought a friend. Party time, baby!"

There was no reply. Neff knocked again with the same result, then tried the handle. The door was locked. "We could get the key," he muttered. "But why bother?"

The lock was as old and flimsy as everything else in the Pacific Paradise. It gave with a splintering screech when Neff drove his foot against it. "Play hard to get, will you?" he growled, carrying on the fiction he had begun. "You ought to know I don't go for that crap, Debbie."

The charade was wasted. When Gamble switched on the overhead light, a glance around the shabby room informed them that there was no audience for it. Two other doors opened on a small closet and a bath that was only slightly larger. Both were empty. Maggi Lane's suitcase lay unpacked on the old-fashioned metal bed, but its owner had vanished.

"I don't believe it!" Neff declared incredulously. "Damn it to hell, she's got to be here."

Gamble raised one edge of the trailing bedspread. "She is," he said softly. Maggi Lane had not eluded them, after all. The awkwardly sprawled figure remained to attest to the cordon's effectiveness . . . but no net has yet been devised capable of holding the soul.

The deputy coroner estimated that Maggi had died around noon, give or take an hour. But if the time could not be determined accurately, there was no doubt about the cause. The nylon cord which had strangled her was still knotted about her throat, so deeply imbedded in the flesh as to be nearly invisible. Death had come fairly rapidly but not—to judge by the contorted face, the bulging eyes and protruding tongue—painlessly. Since there was no sign of a struggle, it seemed likely that Maggi had known her killer and had welcomed him to the room, never suspecting his intentions.

"Must be as strong as an ox," the coroner speculated. "The cord practically decapitated her. And I'd say he's left-handed, too, the way the knot's tied."

Neither fact was of any immediate help in identifying the strangler. Fingerprints, which would have helped, were absent; apparently, the man had worn gloves. A glove was actually found in the room, in fact, seemingly left behind by accident, since its mate was missing. Unfortunately, it was a common make, used by many types of workmen and purchasable in any department store. But since it was the only lead he had, Gamble put it in his pocket, anyway.

By doing so, he was guilty of concealing evidence from the police, but he reasoned that his need was the greater. He was not ready to take the local authorities into his confidence. Nor was he required to. The homicide detectives who responded to the call accepted his nearly true explanation that he and Neff were federal agents who had followed the dead woman in the hope she might lead them to stolen government property, nature unspecified. Since he could not (quite truthfully, in this case) furnish them with the name of her slayer, they did not delve further. They dealt with murder on a daily basis. The death of a supposed prostitute did not inspire them to do more than follow the proscribed routine.

"Probably tried to hold out on her pimp," one of them

surmised. "We'll ask around. Soon as we find out who he is, we'll have your man."

Gamble could only wish that it might prove that easy. "They outguessed us," he told Neff during the long gloomy return to the city.

"Us?" Neff echoed bitterly. "Don't include me."

"All right—they outguessed me. There's no way they could have known we were running Maggi. But the fact that we turned her loose must have worried them. They didn't have any further use for her, anyway, so they decided to get rid of her."

"It's a little late to think of that, isn't it? What it adds up to is that you blew another one, Gamble. God, we had Maggi right in our mitts and you let her go!"

"Tactically, it was the right move. The outcome doesn't change that." But the defense sounded weak even in his ears. Success was all that counted. No amount of rationalization, however valid, could make defeat more palatable. "The game's not over. We'll get them next time."

"What makes you think there's going to be a next time?" Neff replied. Then he snorted. "Forgive me. I'm forgetting your famous intuition."

The
Tracks

THE MEN who gathered in his office the next morning had learned of the fiasco. That, coming on the heels of the earlier disappointment, produced an air of gloom. The euphoria generated by Gamble's confident assumption of command had dissipated noticeably.

"I'm not going to try to kid you," Gamble told them. "Maggi Lane was our best—in fact, our only—lead and losing her is a major setback. I take full responsibility for it."

"Anybody can make a mistake," Roy McElwaine murmured. That was the strongest endorsement he got; the others maintained a careful silence. And even McElwaine added a qualification. "Maybe you should have consulted the rest of us before you stuck your neck out."

"It wouldn't have changed my decision, Mac. I value your input but, in the final analysis, I've got to rely on my own judgment."

Donald Peterson said, "Personally, I find your willingness

to shoulder the blame refreshing. But it doesn't obscure the fact that we seem to be back at square one."

"I don't think that's entirely accurate, Don. While we got a lot less than I hoped for from Maggi, we did get something. For one thing, we know definitely now that the hijackers are holed up somewhere in the L.A. area. That narrows the search a little. For another . . . I want you to look at some movies."

The film, hastily processed during the night, was the photographic record of everyone who had entered or left the Pacific Paradise Hotel during the lengthy stakeout. "The coroner puts the time of death around noon, give or take an hour, so we'll concentrate on the period between eleven A.M. and one P.M. One of the men you'll see is Maggi's killer. If we can figure out which one, maybe we'll be able to salvage something, after all."

The footage was in black-and-white, bore no accompanying sound track and would win no prizes for artistry. From first frame to last, the camera remained fixed on the entrance to the Pacific Paradise. Against this monotonous backdrop, the unknown—and unknowing—actors paraded on and off the stage. Some of the men came boldly in search of the hotel's tawdry pleasures, a larger number with a certain furtiveness. A few got as far as the doorway, then hesitated and departed without entering. This minority could be readily eliminated. But among the majority which remained, no obvious candidate emerged. The clock superimposed in the upper right-hand corner of the film read twelve-twenty before Gamble saw something which caused him to lean forward. "Stop the film," he ordered. "Let's look at that guy again."

They did so. "Notice anything about him?" Gamble asked.

"You mean the way he walks?" McElwaine ventured.

"Yeah. He doesn't hold his arms close to his sides, the way you and I do. They're out a little from the body, making the elbows wider than the shoulders. That's characteristic of weight lifters. Pumping iron causes an enlargement of the latissimus dorsi muscles. And since we're looking for an exceptionally powerful man . . ."

On the screen the burly figure stood frozen, one hand on the doorknob, face turned over his shoulder toward the unseen camera. "What else do you see?"

"A pair of gloves. In his rear pocket."

"In his left rear pocket," Gamble amplified. "Which could mean he's left-handed. Let's skip ahead a bit and see whether we can still spot those gloves when he leaves the hotel."

The audience watched in intent silence until—seventeen minutes later, according to the superimposed clock—the big man emerged from the Pacific Paradise. His manner was as casual as before; there was nothing in his expression to suggest that he might have, moments earlier, snuffed out a woman's life.

They crowded closer to the screen to study the frozen magnified image. "The angle's bad," McElwaine murmured, "but it seems to me that he may only have one glove now."

"I'll guess that he put on the gloves to do his dirty work. Then he stuck them back in his hip pocket. One of them fell out and he never noticed. That wouldn't stand up in court, but it'll do for our purpose. Gentlemen, I believe that's our strangler. Now all we have to do is find him." Gamble smiled wryly. "If we can't recognize him from his picture, maybe we'll know him by his smell. Look for a guy who stinks of formaldehyde. The lab tells me the glove he dropped was saturated with it."

Further analysis of the film indicated that the suspect stood six feet four inches in height, weighed approximately two hundred and fifty pounds, and had a pronounced strabismus of the right eye. The swarthy skin and straight black hair suggested a Latin heritage. While various computers digested this information, Nerk agents began a canvass of gyms, health spas and physical culture establishments in the Los Angeles area.

But before the investigation could produce results, Gamble had a surprise visitor. General Womack flew in from Washington, unannounced, and summoned Gamble to meet him at the airport. "Ostensibly, I'm just passing through on my way down to Palm Springs. A little vacation, if anyone asks. Actually, I needed to talk to you, Gus."

Since they were in almost daily communication via telephone, Gamble was puzzled. "Something wrong, General?"

Womack hesitated. "How are you hitting it off with Kenny Neff?"

"Like a bad marriage. We're staying together for the sake of the children."

"Then I've got news for you. Neff wants a divorce. He claims you've bungled the investigation badly. That he could have wrapped this thing up if it hadn't been for you."

"He's entitled to his opinion."

"Is he right, Gus?" Womack asked searchingly. "Have you bungled the investigation? This business with the Lane woman . . . That wasn't the sort of mistake I expect from you."

"I took a calculated risk. I believed it was worth taking."

"But wouldn't it have been wiser to employ more orthodox methods?"

"Looking back, sure. But when I had to make the decision, I didn't have that privilege. I've never been much for playing the game by the book. You knew that when you called me in. As a matter of fact, isn't that why you called me in?"

"I'm not trying to second-guess you," Womack said un-

78

comfortably, although he obviously was. "Try to understand the spot I'm on. My phone never stops ringing. Last night it was the President himself, wanting to know what progress we're making. I had to tell him we're still playing catch up. Then he asked who I had running the show and did I have complete confidence in you. The way he said it made me wonder if somebody had put a bug in his ear. I did tell you that Neff's uncle is Chairman of the Senate Atomic Energy Commission, didn't I?"

"Did you come out here to fire me, General?"

Womack's failure to reply immediately was evidence that the idea had at least occurred to him. "You haven't gotten the results I hoped you would," he muttered, "but I'm not ready to give up on you. I keep remembering how damned lucky you were—"

"I was never lucky," Gamble contradicted. "I had better than average instincts and I wasn't afraid to trust them. That's all the so-called Gamble magic ever amounted to. That, and being too confounded stubborn to know when I was licked."

"Is the magic still there, Gus? That's what I've got to know."

"A little rusty, maybe, but it's still there. If I didn't think so, I'd be the first to admit it. I don't need this job, General. I've got another one waiting for me."

Womack nodded, his expression relieved. "I guess what I really wanted was a feeling from you that you're still on top of your game. Let the others bitch as much as they like. The job's yours until a better man comes along."

While this was scarcely an unqualified vote of confidence, Gamble accepted it. Womack's insecurity was understandable. He was under tremendous pressure to produce results, harried from above and criticized from below. Little wonder that in the midst of this turmoil he would clutch Gamble like

79

a talisman, unable to believe fully in its powers but unwilling to cast it aside, just in case . . .

"In the meantime," Womack continued, "what are we going to do about Neff? Now that he's gone over your head —you might even say behind your back—it's not reasonable to expect that you can continue working together. Any suggestions—short of kicking him out on his keister?"

"If you can't kick him out, kick him up. The first rule of bureaucracy. Kenny's just itching to prove that the hijacking was the work of a Communist conspiracy. So let him try. Give him a new title—Chief of Task Force Alpha or something that sounds important. Have him report directly to you . . . and turn him loose. That way, he's out of my hair and you can't be accused of not employing his immense talent to the fullest."

"Not bad," Womack agreed with a grin. "But I'm surprised at you, Gus. I thought a Christian was supposed to love his enemies."

"I do," Gamble replied blandly. "Would I recommend him for a promotion if I didn't?"

If Neff suspected that his new assignment was designed to bury him, he showed no resentment. His attitude, rather, was one of vindication. "About time the old man wised up that your by-guess-and-by-God methods aren't getting us anywhere," he told Gamble in parting. "Maybe they worked in the old days, but this is a different ball game."

"Where are you going?" Gamble asked, more from politeness than because he really cared; he would not miss his opinionated rival.

"Where I should have gone in the first place," Neff replied cryptically. "Don't worry. You'll be hearing from me." It had the sound of a threat but Gamble didn't take it seriously. He had more important matters to ponder.

The search for Maggi Lane's suspected slayer did not succeed in netting its quarry. However, his photograph was identified with surprising rapidity. Not just one but several law enforcement agencies were well acquainted with him. His real name (he had used several) appeared to be Tomás Yvarra. Like his victim, he was a native of Puerto Rico. Unlike her, he had spent a good deal of his life in jail for crimes ranging from aggravated assault to armed robbery. His most recent conviction—significantly—stemmed from the holdup of an armored bank truck. Yvarra had served his time in the men's reformatory at Chino. But not all of it; in early January, he had escaped.

Yvarra had apparently lost no time taking up his interrupted career. Less than a month after his escape, a man answering to his description had been one of four who had robbed a savings and loan in West Los Angeles of over $40,000. Nor was that all. A .45 automatic pistol found in the abandoned getaway car provided a link to yet another crime, the looting a week earlier of a National Guard armory in nearby Riverside. Gamble was not surprised to learn, from the inventory supplied by Colonel Mulkey, that the haul included a 60 mm. cannon designed for antitank use and a quantity of plastic explosive.

The pieces of the puzzle were beginning to come together, although the largest piece of all was still missing. Tomás Yvarra was not married, had no living relatives and, according to his record, had never been affiliated with any recognizable gang or criminal organization; he had always worked alone. Now, apparently, the lone wolf had decided to run with a pack. Since Yvarra had spent the past four years in prison, Gamble suspected that he knew where the pack had been formed.

The men's reformatory at Chino was, by American penal standards, an enlightened institution in that it did not resemble the conventional stereotype of a penitentiary. In appearance, it was more like a military post, enclosed with stout chain-link fencing rather than towering stone walls. Absent, too, were the usual cell-blocks. In their place stood squat barracks. Trees dotted the spacious compound; there were flower beds also and a picnic area suitable for family visitation. In prison parlance, Chino was known as "the country club" and its inmates were drawn from among those the system judged to require less restraint than the felons lodged in the maximum security facilities at San Quentin or Folsom.

In the case of Tomás Yvarra, the system's judgment had proved faulty.

"Sure, we blew one," acknowledged the warden, a refreshingly blunt-spoken veteran penologist whose name was Volker. Since Volker's office was being repainted, he sat with Gamble at one of the picnic tables in the shade of a Brazilian pepper tree. His dress was as informal as his manner. Save for the identification badge pinned to his shirt, there was little to distinguish him from his charges who roamed freely about the large compound. "We don't claim to be infallible. We have to go by what we see. It looked to us like Yvarra had gotten his act together—so I guess it's fair to say we were careless."

"How did he bust out? Did he have help?"

"Smuggled himself out in a TV sound truck. One of the local channels was going a piece on our rehabilitation program." Volker shook his head ruefully. "They got a better story than they expected. But they didn't set it up, if that's what you mean. I don't believe anybody set it up, actually. I think it was a spur-of-the-moment thing. Yvarra saw his chance and he took it. Stupid of him, too. He'd have been out in a year, two at the most."

"I'm working on the theory that he was needed outside for a job that couldn't wait that long."

"Needed by whom?"

"You tell me. The rest of my theory is that the job was planned right here. It wouldn't be the first time that's happened. So who did Yvarra pal around with? Was he a member of any clique or gang inside Chino?"

"We have gangs here at Chino, same as every prison. Black, Chicano, Aryan Brotherhood—"

"Puerto Rican?"

"That's one we don't have. And I doubt that Yvarra would have joined it if we did. He was a loner, just him and his barbells. Unless you want to count Brother Stone's Fife and Drum Corps."

"Who's Brother Stone? Your social director?"

Volker laughed. "Hardly. I don't know what you'd call him exactly. Our volunteer fireman, I guess. Simon Stone is a former Catholic priest. He and the church had a falling-out a while back. Went into social work. That got him involved in the problems of the ex-con and he started running a halfway house. About a year ago he came to me and suggested that we set up a retraining program here—individual counseling, group therapy, that sort of thing—to help get the short-timers ready for the street."

"I thought you were already doing that."

"Sure, but we're always short-handed. We can use all the help we can get. Especially help that'll work for nothing. Not only that, there's an advantage to using someone not closely identified with the prison establishment. The men seem to respond to him better."

"How did Yvarra respond?"

"Like everyone. Simon has a gift, there's no other word for it, of reaching these men, even the hard core like Yvarra. I don't know what he did that was different but, whatever it was, it worked. They'd do damn near anything he asked. I could name you a dozen men he turned around completely.

As far as I know, Yvarra is the first one of his flock to go sour. And maybe even he'd have turned out all right too, if Simon hadn't been forced to leave us."

"What forced him? Politics?"

"Health. Simon's got amyotrophic lateral sclerosis, Lou Gehrig's disease—if you're old enough to remember who Lou Gehrig was. He already had it when he started here but he was managing to cope. But around Christmas the doctor ordered him to pack it in. A goddam shame. I really miss that man." Volker nodded in the direction of the barracks. "And so do they."

Gamble agreed that it was, indeed, a shame. "But getting back to Yvarra . . . what made him a special case?"

"Who said he was?"

"You did, more or less. You told me that Stone counseled the short-timers. Yvarra had over a year to serve."

Volker shrugged. "I let Simon pick his own people, more or less. If he heard of someone who might benefit from the experience, I didn't put any artificial restrictions in the way."

"I'd like to talk with Stone," Gamble said. "He seems to have known Yvarra better than most. Maybe he can tell me something about him that will help. Do you think he's well enough?"

"I'm sure he'd be happy to see you. I can give you the address of his halfway house—although I can't promise you'll find him there. The last time I spoke to him, about a month ago, he said something about maybe going to Europe for treatment. He may have left already."

"I didn't think there was any treatment for his disease."

"There isn't. But Simon isn't a man who takes no for an answer." Volker dug out his wallet. "I think I have his card. Yeah, here it is. Seven sixteen Oliver Court. That's in Hermosa Beach, south of—" He broke off to regard his visitor curiously. "Something wrong?"

84

"On the contrary," Gamble said huskily. "For the first time in days, something is very, very right."

Oliver Court. A man using that name had stayed at the Desert Sands Resort in Barstow immediately prior to the hijacking. A preliminary check had failed to locate him. Following the Jeffords-Johnson fiasco, that line of investigation had been allowed to languish. Gamble ordered it revived.

Hermosa Beach lay southwest of Los Angeles, one of a score of oceanfront communities bordering the Pacific from Malibu to San Diego. In Spanish, the name meant "beautiful" and once, no doubt, had been deserved. Uncontrolled growth and a flabby building code plus the failure of the State, until recently, to protect its shoreline from commercial exploitation made the description more a sarcasm than an actuality. As a final indignity, a huge power generating station nearby, oil-fueled, belched forth enough pollution to make the area among the smoggiest in all California.

Although Oliver Court, the man, remained among the missing, Gamble had no difficulty in locating the street which bore that name. It lay in the heart of what had originally been a residential district, long since rezoned. Most of the early family dwellings had been replaced; those which remained had been remodeled. The two-story brown house at 716 was among the latter. It dated from before World War I and was built in midwestern fashion, with a large porch from which to enjoy the nonexistent twilight and a pitched roof to shed the never-falling snow. Over the years it had harbored a number of small, and apparently unprofitable, enterprises. The latest had been Simon Stone's halfway house for ex-convicts.

Now it was empty again. Gamble found a cleanup crew hard at work, supervised by the rental agent, a jovial white-

85

haired man named Osborn. Osborn was disappointed to learn that his visitor had no interest in acquiring the property, but was willing to chat, anyway.

"You just missed him," he informed Gamble. "Stone notified us a month ago that he was going to have to fold his operation. We agreed to let him stay on a week-to-week basis. Yesterday he dropped off the key." Osborn was genuinely regretful. Stone had been an ideal tenant, by which he meant that he paid his rent and caused no problems. "Some people didn't like the idea of having a bunch of ex-cons living here, but Stone kept them in line. Never had a bit of trouble."

"How many were there altogether?"

"Oh, it varied. Sometimes more, sometimes less. I'd guess that, toward the end, there weren't more than three or four." Osborn did not know the names of those three or four nor did he recognize any of the photographs which Gamble had secured at Chino. "Tell you the truth, I didn't come here often. I meet enough crooks, anyway, without having to go looking for them."

Had Stone left a forwarding address? No; it was Osborn's understanding that he was leaving on a trip. "I sure hope it wasn't a long trip. That hearse of his would never make it."

"Hearse?"

"Yeah. This place used to be a mortuary. When it went broke, they auctioned off the equipment and the furnishings. Stone bought a lot of stuff, including the meat wagon. One of those old black Caddies, about a mile long. Me, I wouldn't have taken the thing as a gift even if it had been in good shape, which it wasn't. I figure I'm going to have to ride in one of them soon enough, anyway."

Gamble requested permission to look around. Now that he knew the building had been a mortuary, he saw ample evidence of its previous use. The wall between the parlor and the dining room had been removed to provide a chapel; the

86

carpet bore marks to show where the pews had stood. The large basement, unusual for California, had served for embalming, storage and other functions which the trade euphemistically referred to as "preparation." What use Simon Stone had put it to was impossible to ascertain. However, the lack of dust and debris testified that it had been used. The windowless vault was as immaculate as an operating room.

Afterward, he stood for a while on the porch, deep in thought. Had he pursued another will-o'-the-wisp, reached another dead end? The evidence suggested that he had. There was nothing to connect Simon Stone—former priest, admired social worker, by all accounts a good and honorable man—and his flock of ex-convicts with the bloody ambush in the Mojave Desert. Nothing save a name on a registration card . . . and his own intuition.

The name might be nothing more than a coincidence; such things happened. And so that left only his intuition, a pervasive uneasiness he could neither defend nor dismiss. However, Gamble realized that he could not afford another mistake. His credibility was already being questioned, his competence assailed. That aside, he dared not squander what little time remained by leading his forces into a blind alley.

"Leave no stone unturned," he muttered. That had been his own dictum; it seemed almost prophetic. Faced with a stone named Simon, he could do no less than turn it.

"Simon Stone?" repeated Francis Inman. "Sure, I remember him well. Why are you interested in him, of all people?"

"I was hoping you wouldn't ask," Gamble replied. "Because now I've got to tell you that it's none of your business."

"Is that any way to speak to your elders and—if I may be permitted the vanity—betters?" Inman reproved with a smile.

The stubby priest, cherubic of face and white of hair, was

indeed Gamble's senior in age by fifteen years. In terms of service, his advantage was far greater. This, plus the fact that he held the prestigious post of chancellor of the largest Jesuit college in the southwest, entitled him to deference. But Inman, secure in himself and his God, demanded none. Even if his order had permitted more exalted titles, he still would have chosen to be addressed simply as Father Frank. To Gamble, Inman was more than his ecclesiastical superior. He was also his most trusted friend.

Inman, for his part, regarded his subordinate with affection mixed with a certain amount of misgivings. He alluded to those misgivings now by adding, "Of course, what can you expect of a cop turned priest? Or should that be the other way around?"

"I understood you gave permission for me to labor outside the bounds."

"So I did, Gus. And for the same reason that I gave you permission to deal blackjack in Las Vegas—because I sensed that the Lord was telling me to." He eyed Gamble thoughtfully. "I only hope that I got the message straight. How's it going so far?"

"Not so well that I couldn't use some help." Inman knew only that Womack had requested him on a matter of urgent national security. Gamble thought it better to leave it at that. "Tell me about Simon Stone."

"My information isn't terribly up to date, I'm afraid. I haven't seen Simon for several years. He served as my secretary, you know. He accompanied me to Vatican Two, then stayed on in Rome another year to study and write. You may have read some of his stuff in seminary, his treatise on the catacomb of San Callisto, for example—one of the finest illuminations of the tribulations of the early church I've ever seen. I've got it around here someplace, if you're interested."

Gamble shook his head. "I'll pass on the treatise. I want

to hear about the author."

"If I had to sum him up in one word, that word would be 'genius.' A first-rate mind—coupled with a determination that was almost frightening. There was absolutely nothing he wouldn't try or couldn't do, once he was convinced of its rightness. We all stood a bit in awe of him, I think. I believe that, if things had turned out differently, he might have been our youngest cardinal." Inman sighed. " 'Might have been.' Whittier was right. The saddest words in the language."

"What caused him to demit the priesthood?"

"Simon was like a meteor flashing through the skies, a marvel to behold. But meteors burn out. So do men."

"Do you mind being a little less metaphorical and a little more specific?"

"Just as I suspected, there's no poetry in you," Inman replied with a smile. "All right, to put it in terms you'll understand, Simon suffered a mental breakdown. The medical diagnosis was paranoid schizophrenia."

"What form did it take?"

"Simon held an idealized vision of the church which, I'm sorry to say, didn't always mesh with reality. The church may be ordained by God, but it is administered by men, human beings with human frailties. Simon never really understood that. He saw things in absolutes, black or white, never gray. Accommodation, compromise, gradualism . . . those were dirty words to him. 'I bring not peace but a sword.' That was his credo. Anyone who disagreed with him, even mildly, was not merely mistaken. He was corrupt, a Pharisee, a whited sepulcher. For a while, we put this down to the intolerance of youth. Because of his undeniable brilliance, we excused it. We told ourselves that he'd learn. We didn't realize that he was a sick man."

"At what point did you realize it?"

"Far later than we should have," Inman admitted. "Following his time in Rome, the Society dispatched Simon to South America to gain broader experience. It was an unfortunate decision. He was appalled by the conditions he found there, the poverty, the squalor, the immense gap between the rich and the poor. He was even more appalled by what he conceived to be the church's refusal to do anything about it. He made no secret of it. He demanded that—in his words—the unholy alliance of church and state be ended. The truth is that the church is doing a great deal to alleviate conditions throughout Latin America by exerting its moral authority. But you don't change a culture overnight. Simon wouldn't buy that. Evolution wasn't good enough. Nothing short of revolution would do. When the church declined to rush to the barricades with him, he accused it of sinning against both God and man. We told him to cool it. He wouldn't. Instead, he took it as his mission to mount a one-man reform campaign. Speaking, writing, organizing demonstrations against the system. That brought him into contact with the radical activists. From them, he learned a new theology—what someone has called the theology of terror. The end justifies the means. Violence, sabotage, even murder is acceptable as long as it accomplishes the objective."

"That's interesting," Gamble murmured. "Did he actually participate in any terrorist activities?"

"No, although it might eventually have come to that. Luckily, it never did. Simon had made himself persona non grata with nearly everyone. His visa was revoked and he was sent home to California."

"And defrocked?"

Inman shook his head. "We still had hopes at that point that we'd be able to straighten him out. That what had happened down south was only a temporary aberration. But Simon's psychosis was firmly in the saddle by that time. He saw himself, not as a sheep gone astray, but as the target of a monstrous conspiracy to shut him up. He, and not the church, possessed the only true vision—and it, and not he, should repent."

"How?"

"Oh, he had it very clear in his own mind. The church should purge itself, beginning with its worldly assets. Everything was to be sold or liquidated—land, buildings, stocks, securities, anything that had a dollar value—and the proceeds used to feed the hungry and to aid the oppressed to throw off their chains. Only in this way could the church be rid of corruption and become the revolutionary force Jesus charged it to be."

"That doesn't sound so crazy to me, Father Frank. I've heard worse than that right here on this campus." Gamble added slyly, "Maybe even right here in this office."

"Certainly, the church is wealthy," Inman agreed. "Some might claim that it's too wealthy to fit the suffering servant role. But Saint Paul did not condemn money, only the love of it. Used properly, money can be a marvelous force for good and I believe that, by and large, we are using it properly. Criticize her as you will, the church has endured for nearly two thousand years. She must be doing something right. And, in any event, you don't cleanse the temple by burning it down." Inman sighed. "Simon couldn't see it that way. He wouldn't bow and the church wouldn't bend. Oddly enough, I think that he was absolutely convinced to the very end that it would."

"The end being, I take it, when he was thrown out on his ass."

"Not even then, actually. When he was stripped of his ecclesiastical rank, authority and function—or thrown out on his ass, if you prefer—Simon still continued the fight. He went public. Newspapers, radio, TV . . . for a time he was the darling of the media. They always love a sensational

91

story, particularly when it involves the church. The Prophet from Pasadena, the maverick priest they couldn't muzzle. But the novelty soon wore off. It was at that point that Simon went completely to pieces."

"In what way?"

"He walked into Cardinal Ball's office one day and demanded a meeting with the Pope. No one less would do. The purpose of the meeting, as I understand it, was to arrange for the Holy Father's abdication. He had a pistol. He was quite calm, they tell me—also quite irrational. Somehow they managed to get the pistol away from him. Fortunately, no one was hurt."

"I'm surprised I didn't hear about it," Gamble said. "It must have been in the papers."

"No, we hushed it up. There was some thought of having him arrested but by then it was obvious to everyone that Simon was mentally ill. He needed to be helped, not punished. And, candidly, the church didn't want to be put in the position of appearing to persecute him. So we agreed not to press charges if he would agree to be institutionalized for treatment. It was the right decision. Simon spent several months in a sanitarium. I'm happy to say that he made a complete recovery."

Gamble stroked his jaw dubiously. "How can you be sure of that, Father Frank? Mental illness is a tricky business."

"All I can tell you is what the psychiatrists told me. That Simon had made an excellent adjustment and that his psychosis, if not removed, was at least controlled." Inman shrugged. "The proof of the pudding is that we haven't heard from him in nearly three years. I consider that pretty strong evidence that Simon has shed his delusions about the church as the enemy of mankind. And that he no longer feels driven to remake the world in his ownimage."

"Want to bet?" Gamble asked softly.

His theory was still too bizarre to be shared. Gamble set his subordinates to work on portions of it without giving any of them a glimpse of the picture forming in his imagination.

The men who had passed through Simon Stone's halfway house on their way from prison to the street were tracked down. Most were now productively employed. All gave the lion's share of the credit to the former priest; they remembered him with an admiration that bordered on hero worship. All, that is, who could be located. Three of Stone's most recent protégés were missing. No one, including their parole officers, had seen them in several weeks.

Simon Stone's personal physician confirmed that his patient was indeed suffering from amyotrophic lateral sclerosis, prognosis negative. Had he advised Stone to seek treatment abroad? On the contrary; given the invariably fatal nature of the disease, the doctor viewed the trip as a waste of money. However, Stone had heard of an Italian—"some quack" in the doctor's less than charitable opinion—who claimed to have achieved miraculous cures. Sorry, he didn't recall the Italian's name or the location of his clinic. Since his advice had been disregarded, he no longer considered Stone his patient.

Gamble spoke next with another of Simon Stone's former physicians. James W. Harley had left the sanitarium to enter private practice, setting up his office in Beverly Hills, an area where, more than most, the treatment of the id and the ego flourished. Although over two years had passed, he remembered Stone well. "Simon was one of my unqualified successes," he explained. "We psychiatrists don't have so many that we're likely to forget one."

"Then you considered him completely cured?"

"You don't cure schizophrenia like you cure pneumonia, Mr. Gamble. If we can identify the source of the psychological disturbance—and if we're lucky—we can frequently reduce the psychosis to manageable size, teach the patient how to cope with it."

"What was the source of Stone's psychological disturbance?"

"His love-hate relationship with the Catholic church. He identified with the church to an unhealthy degree. It eventually came to the point where he believed that he *was* the church. That only he possessed the true vision. That all who failed to share his apocalyptic views—from the Pope on down—were instruments of the devil."

"What sort of treatment did you use?"

"Shotgun. Insulin shock, chemicals, psychotherapy. I don't know which one deserves the most credit. What matters is, Simon got well."

"Is there any danger of a relapse?"

"Of course. It's my opinion that most schizophrenia is environment-induced. Return the patient to the same environment and he may wig out all over again. Severe stress or trauma can have the same effect."

"Severe stress or trauma," Gamble repeated. "Like what, for example?"

"It would vary with the individual. For one man, it might mean the loss of his job, or merely the fear of losing it. For another, the death of a loved one or—"

"How about knowing that you were going to die?"

"Hell, Mr. Gamble, everyone knows he's going to die. I presume you mean knowing when you're going to die." Harley shrugged. "Even the well-integrated personality has difficulty coping with that. In the controlled schizophrenic, it might trigger a relapse."

"If that happened, would it be obvious to people around him?"

"Nonprofessionals, you mean? Maybe yes, maybe no. It

would depend to a great extent on how well you know the subject prior to his illness. Without a basis of comparison, you might consider him to be merely eccentric or 'different.' Few of them fit the raving maniac image. Some are even quite fascinating, attractive people, the life of the party, the type that others gravitate to. But since they're not bound by ordinary moral values, they sooner or later come into conflict with society—with sometimes tragic consequences." He regarded Gamble with a frown. "I assume that your questions have a purpose. Am I also to assume that Simon is in some sort of trouble?"

"I don't know, Doctor. But if he is, then we're all in it with him."

For the next forty-eight hours, Gamble continued to pursue his almost surreptitious investigation while at the same time allowing the others already under way to continue. In response to General Womack's daily (and, sometimes, it almost seemed, hourly) telephone calls, he replied evasively, "I think I may be onto something but I need a little more time."

"We're running out of time," Womack reminded him. "They could have had their bomb four days ago. Can't you give me something solid to pass along upstairs?"

His agitation was increased by the fact that the story was beginning to leak out, an almost inevitable development considering the scope of the search and the number of people involved in it. The first account, luckily, was garbled, merely reporting that an unspecified amount of fissionable material was rumored missing from the Punta Fierro nuclear power generating station. NRC officials, as instructed, had issued a flat denial. However, given the low level of credibility according to government statements these days, the matter would scarcely end there.

Gamble refused to succumb to either panic or pressure.

95

"Tell Washington we're making progress. That will have to satisfy them."

"It won't," Womack predicted dolefully. "Hell, it doesn't even satisfy me."

Yet, even if Gamble had chosen to take him into his confidence, it was unlikely that Womack would have found much to encourage him. The information Gamble sought continued to filter in, a piece at a time, and none of it was conclusive. According to the State Department, Stone had been issued a passport in January; the other missing men had not, at least under their own names. Motor Vehicles reported that, on the same day he vacated the former mortuary, Simon Stone had sold the Cadillac limousine (virtually given it away, in fact) to a wrecking yard in Inglewood. Had he purchased another car to replace it? No, he had not.

To these facts, Gamble added another by simply glancing at the map. The Los Angeles International Airport was also in Inglewood, almost within walking distance—or at least an easy cab ride—of the wrecking yard. He set his agents to checking passenger manifests and was not surprised to learn that Simon Stone had indeed departed, via scheduled airline, for Rome on the day in question.

Alone? That was a question which the airline's district operations officer, a pleasant young executive named Lancaster, wasn't prepared to answer. "According to the manifest, Flight Thirty-two carried three hundred and thirty-nine other SOB's." He added quickly, lest his visitor consider his view of the airline's customers to be less than respectful, "Souls on Board. Your Mr. Stone bought a single ticket. That isn't to say that he wasn't traveling as a member of a party. We just don't have any way of knowing."

None of the other names on the manifest was familiar to Gamble. But names could be falsified and passports could be forged. What about cargo?

Well, that was a different matter, according to Lancaster. "Because of the risk involved—midair explosion or fire, danger to the aircraft—we've got to know what we're carrying. FAA regulations require it. Even if they didn't, common sense would."

"Suppose I wanted to ship something hazardous—explosives, chemicals, radioactive material—and I didn't want you to know it. What's to stop me from putting it in a box, stamping it pineapple juice and slipping it past you?"

"If you shipped pineapple juice with us routinely, you might get away with it. But if you didn't, then you'd have to prove to us that it was actually pineapple juice in the box. Every piece of cargo is visually inspected before it's accepted. If there's any question whatever about the contents, it's opened or X-rayed. We can't afford to take chances. Too many nuts running around."

Flight 32 had carried several tons of air freight in addition to mail and the passengers' baggage, the vast majority of it from reputable commercial shippers. Every item had been certified innocuous. None was registered to Simon Stone or, for that matter, to any of the names on the manifest. Nor did a check of other flights, both scheduled and nonscheduled, leaving for Rome on the same day or subsequently, turn up anything which might conceivably be a bomb or SNM, special nuclear material, the euphemism those who worked with it used to denote weapons-grade plutonium.

Another man, totting up the evidence, might logically have concluded that the negatives far outweighed the positives and so merited no further investigation. Gus Gamble, leaning heavily on his intuition (and, to be truthful, little else), did not. There were still holes in the puzzle, pieces missing and pieces which didn't appear to fit. But he felt that, at last, he saw the picture and saw it whole. He decided that the time had come to unveil it.

"Talk about ESP!" Womack exclaimed. "I was just getting ready to phone you."

"I thought we'd better have a meeting, General."

"Now that's even stranger. I had the same idea. How soon can you get down here?"

"That depends on whether I drive or fly."

"Fly, by all means," Womack ordered decisively. "We'll be waiting for you, Gus."

We? Gamble wondered as he hung up. It was not like Womack to employ the imperial pronoun to refer to himself. His use of it now suggested that he had company. And, furthermore, company that was in his confidence. Since that embraced only a bare handful of high government officials—including the highest official of all—Gamble suspected that he might be required to present his admittedly bizarre thesis to more exalted ears than he had anticipated. The possibility did not dismay him. There was a streak of ham in him; he relished the opportunity to perform and the more distinguished the audience, the better.

The flight to Palm Springs was brief. In barely half an hour, he was transported from the chill and smoggy city over the lofty San Gabriel mountains and deposited in the sparkling desert sunshine. In fact, he spent more time in the taxi which bore him across the valley to Womack's temporary home than aboard the aircraft.

The house belonged to one of Womack's friends, a film director whose profession compelled him to spend most of his time elsewhere. Low and rambling, it perched on the edge of a golf course at the foot of towering Mount San Jacinto, surrounded by a high stucco wall and shaded by trees, cottonwood and tamarisk, which thrived in the arid environment. Elsewhere, it would have been called a mansion, but not here in this affluent community where conspicuous consumption was the norm.

Ashley Womack awaited him in the lanai beside the free form pool, although neither he nor the two men with him were dressed for swimming. Gamble realized immediately that his expectations had been too high. Womack's guests were not top level officials, after all. One was a tall, well-groomed man he had never met before. The other, looking more cheerful than Gamble had ever seen him, was Kenneth Neff.

"Hey, when did you get back?" Gamble asked.

"Flew in last night." Neff indicated his companion. "Shake hands with Nils Berryman."

The name meant nothing to Gamble. But if he did not know Berryman, at least Berryman knew him. "So you're Gamble. I've heard a lot about you." Gamble couldn't decide whether this was intended as a compliment. Berryman's voice was flat, lacking expression. It went with the rest of him; the hawklike face was a mask which concealed rather than revealed its owner's feelings. Although the thin lips smiled, the cold hooded eyes did not. He exuded politeness but not warmth.

Womack interpreted his what's-this-guy-doing-here? glance correctly. "Nils represents the CIA."

"CIA?" Gamble's eyebrows rose. "When did they get in on the act?"

"Kenny will explain."

Neff said quickly, "If you don't mind, General, my explanation can wait. I'm sure that Gamble has something more important to tell you. I'm anxious to hear what it is."

For some unknown reason, the request seemed to make Womack uncomfortable. He frowned, cleared his throat and, finally, shrugged. "If that's agreeable to everyone." He didn't look at Gamble. "Gus, the floor's all yours."

"I'll give you the punch line first," Gamble said. "I believe

I know who hijacked our ploot. I believe I know where they took it in order to build their nuclear device. I believe that device was built—and I believe I know the intended target." He saw Neff and Berryman exchange startled glances and he smiled. "Don't applaud yet, gentlemen. Hold it until I've finished."

"How did you manage to stumble onto it?" Neff asked in a voice which sounded more disappointed than pleased.

"I happened to ask the right question of the right person at the right time. After that, it was just a matter of extrapolating. This isn't an ordinary crime—and the man responsible isn't an ordinary criminal. His name is Simon Stone."

Neff blinked. "Simon who? Never heard of him."

"I'm not surprised. You won't find him in the files because—"

"Who says?" Berryman interrupted, welcoming the opportunity to demonstrate his agency's vaunted omniscience. "Spoiled priest. Got himself in hot water down in Latin America a while back. After you'd left us, Kenny."

"That's right. Stone was eventually defrocked for insubordination. He was a brilliant man—a genius, according to some—who saw himself as the new messiah, sent by God to purify the church of complacency and corruption. The church didn't buy it. To make a long story shorter, Stone went off the deep end and wound up in a sanitarium. Paranoid schizophrenia. After treatment, he was released, apparently cured, meaning that he had renounced his messianic views. Then something happened that caused him to flip all over again. He learned that he was incurably ill. I think this must have struck him as God's terrible rebuke for failing to carry out his appointed mission. So now, in what little time he had left, he would have to make amends. The church had not heeded his warning. The church must be punished. Fire

100

and brimstone—that was the Biblical way of handling it. We don't have much fire and brimstone around these days. But we do have ploot."

"The Mad Priest," Neff murmured. "Or, The Vengeance of Almighty God. Sounds like an old-time melodrama." His words carried mockery but his tone did not. Strangely, he appeared to be intrigued with the story.

"With a difference, Kenny. In the old-time melodramas, the villain usually had to invent his doomsday weapon. Stone didn't have to. We'd invented it for him. All he had to do was to get hold of it. For that, he needed professional help. He went looking for it in the most logical place. He talked his way into a job at Chino as an unpaid counselor. That gave him the perfect opportunity to recruit his disciples, men with special talents and few scruples."

Berryman chuckled. "I suppose you're going to tell us there were twelve of them."

"Nope, only four. Stone was more selective than Jesus. And he had to screen quite a few candidates before he found the four who qualified." Gamble opened his briefcase and removed the photographs it contained. He held up each in turn. "This is Simon Stone, taken several years ago. Looks harmless enough, doesn't he? But study those eyes . . . The rest are mug shots. Burt Troob, former machinist, felony manslaughter. Al Ziegler, ex-Army Special Forces, demolitions specialist, assault with a deadly weapon. George Parker, chemical engineer, second degree murder. And, finally, our old friend Tomás Yvarra, armed robbery. Put them together and what do you have? An engineer, a machinist, an explosives expert and an authority on armored cars. All you need to add is a leader—a man with a plan—and you've got a group peculiarly qualified to hijack the ploot and to do something with it afterward."

"Objection," Berryman said lazily. "What about motive?

Stone may have one that satisfies him, but I can't see four seasoned criminals signing up for his crusade."

"By all accounts, Stone is a magnetic personality, almost hypnotic. But you're right, Berryman. My guess is that he conned them with the promise of a big payoff, big enough to make murder acceptable." Gamble paused. "Let's look at the timetable. Troob, Ziegler and Parker were released from Chino during November and December. They all took up residence at the halfway house Stone had established—but if they made any effort to get jobs, I haven't been able to find out about it. Shortly after they arrived, Stone quit his counseling post at the prison. It had served his purpose. But they couldn't make their move without Yvarra. He busted out of Chino in early January. Three weeks later, the National Guard armory in Riverside was looted and weapons and plastic explosive taken. A week after that, a bank in West L.A. was robbed by four men, one of them identified as Yvarra. Forty thousand bucks, enough for operating expenses, was stolen. Eighteen days later, 319 was hijacked. We estimated it would take two weeks to fabricate the bomb. Well, two weeks and one day following the hijacking, Stone closed his halfway house and the men who had been living there disappeared. I'd say that was a pretty persuasive sequence of events."

Neff pursed his lips, his attitude judiciously impartial as though the matter were only of academic interest. "It's persuasive only if you accept the notion that Stone fits into it. I don't see that you've established that."

"Hear me out, Kenny. Yvarra escaped from prison in a TV sound truck. Stone knows the program manager from the days when he was making the rounds of the talk shows. The program manager recalls that it was Stone who suggested they film a documentary at Chino. That's one link. Here's another. Stone's halfway house in Hermosa Beach was

102

located on Oliver Court. A man named Oliver Court—whom we haven't been able to locate—stayed at the Desert Sands Resort immediately prior to the hijacking. Want more? Okay, Maggi Lane was murdered in Wilmington, which is only a few miles down the freeway from Hermosa Beach. And finally . . . remember the glove Yvarra dropped, the one that had formaldehyde on it? The halfway house was a former mortuary. Formaldehyde is used in embalming. Those gloves probably belonged to the morticians."

Berryman lit a cigarette. The cloud of exhaled smoke made his masklike face even more unreadable. "Since you believe that Stone has his weapon, I assume you also feel you know what he intends to do with it?"

"Use it to force the church to submit to his demands. And if the church refuses—which it will—then use it to wreak his vengeance. Stone is already in Rome."

"And the bomb?"

"It's either there or on its way. I can't tell you yet how he managed to sneak it out of the country. I'm leaving for Rome this evening. With a little luck and some cooperation from the Italian police, I hope I'll be able to prevent the ultimate bang."

Womack, the hitherto silent observer, cleared his throat. "Gus, have you been in touch with the Italians yet?"

"That's my next order of business, General."

"Then it's not too late," Womack said in a relieved voice. "I was afraid you might have put your foot in it."

"You're not suggesting that we don't tell the Italians, are you?"

"It's not actually a suggestion," Womack replied uncomfortably. "It's just that, well, there's no reason to bring them in on it."

"Why not?"

"Allow me, General." Neff had been waiting for this moment. He favored Gamble with a sardonic smile. "I've really got to hand it to you. You came up with a hell of a flashy theory. There's just one tiny flaw in it. It's pure unadulterated horse manure."

There was a moment of silence. Gamble broke it with a chuckle. "What don't you like about my theory, Kenny? Aside from the fact that it's mine."

Womack said, in a voice made husky by embarrassment, "I should have told you on the phone—"

"Maybe you should have, General. But you didn't. Now I get the feeling that I've walked into a brace game." He studied Neff's triumphant expression. "Let's see your hole card, Kenny."

"Aces all the way, Gamble. I may not be a living legend but I at least know how to add up the facts. The biggest fact of all was right there under your nose and you didn't even see it. I could have pointed it out to you but you wouldn't have listened, any more than you listened to me when I wanted to squeeze Maggi Lane. That's too easy, it doesn't have the Gamble flair. You'd rather go chasing psycho priests and dreaming up plots against the Vatican."

Gamble sighed. "All right, I'm not your type. So what else is new?"

"Try this one on for size. Tomás Yvarra. Magdalena Lopez. You're big on links. Do you see one there?"

"Both Puerto Rican, if that's what you mean."

"That's exactly what I mean. The only two people we can definitely connect with the hijack—or to each other—and they're from the same little island."

"I didn't overlook that," Gamble said patiently. "I figure Yvarra probably knew Maggi from the past. That was how Stone recruited her."

"Forget Stone, for Christ's sake!" Neff made an impatient brushing gesture. "This isn't a diabolical scheme dreamed up

104

by a two-bit messiah. It's exactly what I said it was from the beginning, a Communist-inspired and Communist-directed plot against the security of the United States. Ever hear of the FALN?" Gamble nodded but Neff would not forgo the pleasure of elaborating, anyway. "It's an acronym for Armed Forces of Puerto Rican National Liberation. They're a Marxist guerrilla group. Their aim is to drive the United States out of Puerto Rico—and, eventually, out of the hemisphere. Their tactics are all the standard ones—terror, sabotage, subversion, assassination."

"Thanks for the history lesson. But I hope you're not going to suggest that the FALN came all the way up here to hijack our ploot."

Neff gave him the look the initiated reserve for the uninformed. "The FALN is already here. It has been for years. Remember the attempt to assassinate President Truman back in 1950? That was their work. Since then, they've claimed the credit for over twenty-five bombings."

"The FALN was one of the groups the FBI checked out. They came up empty."

"The FBI," Berryman said contemptuously; his tone made it a dirty word. "They may not know—and you obviously don't—but we've known for some time that the FALN was going to try to stage a real spectacular. We had a pretty good idea where—Panama. We weren't sure exactly how . . . but now that question has been answered, too."

"Not as far as I'm concerned. Sorry."

"The Canal, of course. A nuclear device exploded there—aboard a ship passing through, for example—would put the ditch out of commission for months, maybe permanently. A second Pearl Harbor, which would seriously impair our naval capability, not to mention the political and economic consequences."

"You're not really serious, are you? If you are, you don't

105

understand Marxist guerrillas. They don't go for the jugular. They nibble away at their victim a piece at a time, until he bleeds to death—or until he gets so sick of it that he gives them what they want. Blowing up the Canal would be spectacular, all right, but it would also be counter-productive. It would make us so damn mad—and everybody else, too, including Panama—that we'd never stop until we'd wiped them out." Gamble shook his head. "Your Pearl Harbor analogy doesn't hold water, Berryman. Unless, of course, you figure the FALN is just the cat's paw and what we're really facing is the beginning of World War Three."

Berryman smiled enigmatically. "Who knows how deep the roots of this conspiracy go? I've learned from experience not to rule out any possibility, no matter how far-fetched it might seem."

"That's odd. You've apparently ruled out mine."

"Solely on the basis of the evidence. The facts don't support your hypothesis. They do support ours."

"What facts? I haven't heard any yet—except that Yvarra and Maggi Lane both came from Puerto Rico."

"And are believed to have had some connection with the FALN."

"When you say 'believed,' that means you can't prove it. Am I right?"

"The Lopez woman's late husband was a known leftist who worked for Puerto Rican independence, which is a FALN objective. Yvarra, when he first came to the States and before he went to prison, was employed by Apex Exporting."

"I must not have been paying attention," Gamble said. "What's Apex Exporting?"

"Apex is an export brokerage firm which has offices on both coasts and in New Orleans. A certain amount of their business is legitimate, but that's simply a cover for their principal function, which is to funnel illegal shipments of guns and ammunition to the FALN apparatus in Puerto Rico and elsewhere. We've had our eye on them for some time."

"Then why haven't you closed them down?"

"Once you've identified a front operation, it's sometimes more productive to allow it to continue to function—under close surveillance, of course. It allows you to stay one jump ahead of the other side. Staying one jump ahead is often the difference between victory and disaster." Berryman shrugged. "As it was in this case. Yesterday Kenny and I led a raid on the Apex offices and warehouse—"

"Which happens to be located in Wilmington," Neff put in. "Not a few miles down the freeway from Hermosa Beach —but only a couple of blocks from the Pacific Paradise Hotel."

"We arrested the local manager and two of his employees who, so far, have told us nothing of value," Berryman continued. "We also seized Apex's records, which told us a great deal. Three days ago, they shipped several cases of what the manifest described as machine parts on a Liberian freighter, the *Charles E. Moore*. Destination, Maracaibo, Venezuela." He smiled. "By way of the Canal."

Neff, unhappy out of the spotlight, took advantage of the pause. "The bomb was fabricated right there in the Apex warehouse. They have all the tools and equipment necessary to do the job, plus the privacy to do it in. Who pays attention to what goes on inside a warehouse? Once the bomb was built, it was the simplest thing in the world to crate it, label it machine parts and ship it out on the freighter."

Gamble waited politely. When it appeared that Neff had finished, he asked, "Is that all?"

"Yes. No. You mentioned the formaldehyde. It's not only used in mortuaries. Have you forgotten that formalin is a prime ingredient for RDX? You need a powerful explosive to trigger the nuclear reaction and RDX certainly qualifies."

"So does TNT—which is easier to get and safer to handle. Why should anyone run the risk of manufacturing RDX when they don't have to?"

"I don't know why they did it," Neff said stubbornly. "I just know that they did it."

"I hate to disagree with you, Kenny, but you don't really *know* anything. This strikes me as typical CIA baloney, where the facts are made to fit the theory, rather than the other way around. You wanted this to be a Communist plot. So you went to the people who deal in them and, sure enough, they found one that would do."

Berryman's smile was patronizing. "Do I seem to detect a note of jealousy?"

"You bet you do," Neff said. "That's the trouble with getting an inflated reputation. Pretty soon you start to believe it yourself."

"My reputation, inflated or otherwise, isn't the question. If I thought you were right, I'd be the first one to cheer. But you're not."

"Would you care to put it to a vote?"

Gamble turned toward Womack. "You've heard both sides. I'm not asking you to make a choice. I am asking you to keep an open mind until all the facts are in. That freighter will be arriving off Panama within a couple of days. Okay, board and search her before she enters the Canal. If they find the ploot, then I'm the biggest jackass in the country. But in the meantime, I'm off to Rome to track down Simon Stone and—" He broke off, unable to believe that Womack was shaking his head.

"I'm sorry, Gus. The facts are already in. Kenny's right and you're wrong."

"What do you mean? He's got no proof, not yet."

108

"Don't I?" Neff laughed gleefully, relishing the opportunity to administer the coup de grace. "Read 'em and weep, Gamble. After what we turned up at Apex, I asked the Mexican Coast Guard to keep an eye on the *Charles E. Moore,* to make sure we didn't lose her. I heard from them this morning, just before I hotfooted it down here. They reported that the ship blew up last night off the tip of Baja California."

Gamble's mouth felt suddenly dry. "Blew up? How?"

"How do you think? There's a storm down south, what they call a chubasco, so visual surveillance was impossible. But the ship all of a sudden went off the radar. When the Mexicans investigated, they couldn't find a trace of her." Neff shrugged. "It's obvious what happened. The bastards built a faulty bomb and it went off in their faces."

"What about fallout?" Gamble asked huskily.

"Don't you suppose I thought about that? Our planes made a sweep of the area and, sure enough, they found upper atmosphere radioctivity. Not as much as you might expect, granted, but the storm probably dispersed a lot of it." Neff regarded him with a satisfaction he made no attempt to hide. "Are you ready for the vote now?"

Ashley Womack watched his luncheon guest toy morosely with his salad. "Don't take it so hard," he advised. "You win some and you lose some." The winners had departed in triumph; the loser remained by invitation. "What really counts is that we're out from under. This could have turned into a terrible tragedy. We're just mighty lucky that it didn't, and I thank God for it." He winked, an expression of high good humor. "That is, if you don't mind my muscling in on your territory."

"Why should I mind? Everybody seems to be doing it."

"Look, I know you're as sore as hell at Neff for rubbing

your nose in it the way he did. I suspect you're sore at me, too, for not stopping him. I can't blame you. I was so damn grateful to him for getting the monkey off my back that I let him have his way. I allowed him to walk all over you. I'm sorry, Gus. I owed you something better than that."

Gamble could not dispute it. Womack's weakness, his willingness to leave his friend perched serenely on the end of a limb while others sawed it off, had hurt him greatly. Yet K. K. Hartman had warned him. The old man was but a shadow of his former self, a tired warrior who yearned only to close his distinguished career with one final victory—or, at the very least, to avoid an ignominious defeat. He had already antagonized the ambitious Neff by installing Gamble as his superior. To make amends for the tactical error and regain a seat on the bandwagon, he had been compelled to countenance Gamble's humiliation . . . and auld lang syne be damned.

But since recriminations would change nothing, he let Womack off the hook with a shrug. "Kenny was bound and determined to collect his pound of flesh. That doesn't bother me. What does bother me is that he may have collected prematurely."

"Oh, come on, Gus. Sour grapes—that's not your style."

"Isn't there any doubt in your mind at all, General?"

"Put aside your prejudice for a moment if you can and consider the facts." Womack ticked them off on his bony fingers. "We know that Tomás Yvarra—and possibly the Lane woman—had some prior connection with the FALN. We know that the FALN was planning some skulduggery. We know that Apex Exporting is a FALN front. We know that Apex shipped something aboard the *Charles E. Moore*. We know that the ship blew up—and that we've found upper level radioactivity. It all adds up, Gus."

"Maybe. But I can't shake the feeling, down deep in my

110

gut, that it adds up wrong."

"What have you got that's better?" Womack countered patiently. "An ex-priest who may or may not be a dangerous psychopath, who may or may not have a grudge against the Catholic church and who may or may not have used his position at Chino to recruit a gang of cutthroats. Even if it's all true—and God knows you haven't proved it—what earthly logic justifies your assumption that he's guilty of hijacking our ploot?"

"You're forgetting the Oliver Court connection."

"How much does that amount to, really? You haven't tied Simon Stone to Oliver Court—aside from the fact that he lived on a street with that name. For that matter, you haven't actually tied Oliver Court to the hijacking. If there is a connection, as you seem to believe, I'll give you Tomás Yvarra. He could have known the address of Stone's halfway house. When he needed an alias, he borrowed the name."

"I suppose it's possible," Gamble conceded. "However—"

"However, nothing! The clincher to me is that your theory doesn't account for the ploot and Neff's does. He can show it moving logically from the Mojave to the Apex warehouse to the freighter and finally, boom! But you . . . If Stone did build a bomb, what the hell happened to it? It wasn't in his house, it wasn't in his car and—unless the airlines are in cahoots with him—it wasn't in his luggage, either. So where is it?"

Gamble traced a meaningless design on the tablecloth with his spoon. "Somehow he managed to get the bomb aboard that flight or another one. There's no other answer."

"There is another answer, but you're too pigheaded to accept it. Stone isn't involved. There's not one single solitary piece of hard evidence that he ever was."

"That doesn't make my feeling go away, General."

"Try an Alka-Seltzer. Gus, you gave it your best shot and

you missed. You're only making yourself ridiculous by continuing to bang away with an empty gun." Womack sighed. "It's time you faced up to reality. You leaned too heavily on your intuition—and, for once, it let you down."

"Wait a minute," Francis Inman interrupted, rummaging in his desk. "I must have one around here somewhere."

"What are you looking for?"

"A crying towel. You obviously need it."

"Thanks," Gamble said sourly. "Spoken like a true friend."

"What do you want from me, Gus?"

"A little counsel and advice, I guess."

Inman shook his head slowly. "I think not. I think you're really hoping I'll tell you that why, of course, you're right—and everyone else is wrong!"

Gamble managed a grudging smile. "All contributions gratefully accepted."

"You're expecting me to express an opinion on a matter outside my ken. I'm simply not qualified to judge. Even worse, you're asking me to override the opinion of men who are qualified, professionals in their field."

"Each of whom has his own ax to grind," Gamble argued. "Neff has eyes for being Numero Uno. This is going to clinch it for him. Berryman—he's the typical CIA Cold Warrior with Oak Leaf Cluster. And Womack . . . the General's burned out. All he wants is peace with honor."

"And Gus Gamble?" Inman inquired shrewdly. "What's driving him?"

"Fear. I'm scared that Neff's pat solution is mistaken—and what the consequences will be if it is."

"Are you sure about that? Search your heart, Gus. Are you afraid of the consequences—or are you afraid you're

112

going to have to admit that Super Cop has lost some of his old magic?"

"You're suggesting that it's just my ego at work?"

"You're the only one who can answer that. But it does seem to me that you've allowed yourself to become emotionally involved, perhaps above and beyond the call of duty. I'm aware of your past reputation. The young wizard, the infallible hunter—"

"I buried that guy a long time ago, Father Frank."

"Did you?" Inman pursed his lips. "I wonder if we can ever entirely escape our past. I've had this concern about you —that deep down you're still more cop than priest. There's no shame attached to it. Some men are meant to be shepherds, some are meant to be hunters. Have you been deluding yourself the past few years as to which is your proper role?"

"I took this job under duress and that's the truth."

"It may be the truth—but it isn't necessarily the answer. I suspect that you've thoroughly enjoyed getting back into the thick of battle, the chance to take up the challenge and prove that you're still the best. I look at you now and what do I see? A dedicated priest grateful to be allowed to return to his parish? Nope. I see a thoroughly disgruntled man, a lover whose mistress has left him for another guy."

Gamble hesitated, not relishing the picture Inman drew but unable to reject it out of hand. Did his stubbornness spring, as he proclaimed, from a deeply held conviction—or was it rooted in pique? Or, equally serious, in a reluctance to leave the party? "That's a pretty serious charge," he murmured.

"Yes, it is. And I suggest you ponder it seriously. Preferably on your knees. Are you a cop or are you a priest? You can't be both."

113

Gamble sighed. "Okay, Father Frank. I'm beginning to get the message."

"I'd be interested to hear what you think it is."

"That I'm wrong. Everyone else has said so—and now I'll say it, too. I'm finally going to learn to take no for an answer."

Inman regarded him thoughtfully. "I hope you mean it. Ego, excessive pride, the feeling that you're superior to other men may be acceptable in a policeman. It's fatal in a priest. Remember Simon Stone."

"If you don't mind, I'd just as soon forget Simon Stone. I'm going back to Las Vegas. It's a town of losers and I belong. I need one final favor, though. I had to turn in my official car." He mustered a feeble smile. "Along with my legend. So how about driving me to the airport?"

The early evening traffic was, as usual, heavy. These days no one lived within walking distance of where he worked. Los Angeles lacked an adequate public transportation system. As a result, the close of the business day sent a massive transfusion of automobiles into the city's already sclerotic arteries, a torrent of machines which clogged every freeway and boulevard. The torrent sometimes flowed rapidly, more often slowly, occasionally not at all. Drivers, victims of the carburetor culture they had helped to create, endured the ordeal in teeth-clenched silence or relieved its frustration by cursing their fellow victims, both by voice and by horn.

"You're going to miss your flight," Inman fretted; even priests were not immune to irritation. The possibility disturbed him more than his passenger. Now that he accepted defeat, Gamble felt detached, lethargic in spirit and somehow uninvolved in what came next. He closed his eyes, content to let Inman do the worrying, and did not open them even when they left the congested freeway for the boulevard which led to the airport.

114

Los Angeles International is constructed roughly in the shape of a giant horseshoe, its rim composed of runways and taxiways, with the various terminal buildings forming a smaller arc within the larger. All automobile traffic enters and leaves the horseshoe through its mouth to the east, and here Inman encountered still another slowdown.

"Wouldn't you know it?" he grumbled. "First, we hit every red light . . . and now we're stuck behind a funeral procession."

Gamble opened his eyes and saw that they were indeed following a gleaming black automobile which would have been immediately identifiable as a hearse even without a glimpse of its cargo, a bronze casket, ornately fashioned. "The way I feel, I fit right in."

"I've seen corpses who looked more cheerful than you," Inman agreed. He drummed his fingers impatiently on the steering wheel as they pursued the slow-moving automobile around the horseshoe. Only propriety restrained him from sounding his horn. "Well, praise the Lord!"

His gratitude was for the fact that the limousine had finally cleared the path by turning through a gate reserved for freight shipments. With this obstacle removed, Inman accelerated past the legal speed limit and came to a jarring halt outside the terminal which was Gamble's destination. "I think you can still make it. But you'd better hurry."

Gamble grabbed his suitcase. "Thanks for the lift."

Despite his injunction to speed, Inman beckoned him back. "A last word of advice. Snap out of it! Go back to your work, immerse yourself in it and put this disappointment behind you. Or else." His expression was kindly, yet stern. "You can consider that an order, my son."

"Yes, Father, sir," Gamble replied. "I'll be a good boy from now on."

He hastened into the terminal and fell into line at the ticket counter. It occurred to him that, had matters gone as he expected, he would be standing now in another line at another counter, headed for Rome, Italy, rather than Las Vegas, Nevada. Oh, well, there were worse destinations. Far worse, he amended, as he remembered the casket he and Inman had unwillingly followed on its final journey. Depressed he was, but depression passed while death was permanent. He wondered pensively who the casket's unseen occupant had been and to what distant resting place he was to be conveyed, stacked by unfeeling hands in a frigid hold like so much . . .

"Cargo, by God!" His shout caused the woman in line ahead of him to turn, startled by the outburst. Gamble was not aware of her surprised face. His rapt eyes contemplated only the vision forming in his imagination, sharp and clear and terrifying. He struck his forehead with the heel of his hand. "That's it! Dummy, dummy, dummy!"

"Are you all right?" the woman asked curiously.

Her question went unanswered. Gamble was already running for the door, toward the taxis lined up at the curb outside.

Ashley Womack was by nature a social animal, a man who loved good fellowship and good conversation, preferably shared over a good meal. Neither the infirmities of advancing age nor the death of his wife the previous year had succeeded in turning him into a recluse. For the past week, however, he had been a virtual prisoner in Palm Springs, chained to the telephone and seeing no one save his subordinates. With the burden lifted at last, he felt like celebrating. For that, companionship was required. He telephoned several old friends in Los Angeles and arranged a late dinner party at Chasen's.

The meal was excellent, the conversation lively and the

116

laughter frequent. Dessert had not yet been served when a waiter informed the boisterous host that a gentleman was urgently requesting to see him. Womack, mellow from more than the liquor, excused himself, pausing only to order another bottle sent to the table—and to warn the others against consuming it in his absence.

The identity of his unexpected visitor did not dampen his spirits. "Gus!" he cried as if it had been months rather than mere hours since they had parted. "I didn't think you were still in town."

"Sorry to interrupt your party, General."

"You're not interrupting a thing," Womack assured him. "Come on and join us."

"Thanks, but I have to talk to you. Alone." The small foyer, although empty at this late hour, offered little privacy and the bar even less. "Would you mind stepping outside with me for a minute?"

The night was cold after the warmth of the restaurant, the air clammy with fog which limited visibility to a few yards. Along Beverly Boulevard crept the disembodied headlights of automobiles, but on the sidewalk, dimly illuminated by the artificial moon of a sodium vapor lamp, there were no pedestrians. Womack shivered, as much from the change of environment as from the chill. "Why all the mystery, Gus?"

"I've found out how Simon Stone shipped his bomb to Rome."

Womack squinted at him as if he had not heard correctly, then expelled his breath disgustedly. "You mean you dragged me out here . . . Oh, come off it! When are you going to stop beating that dead horse?"

"It's not dead, General." Gamble shook his head ruefully. "I don't know why it took me so long to figure it out. Stone's hideout that used to be a mortuary, the hearse he bought for no good reason—"

"What the hell are you babbling about? Make sense, for God's sake!"

"I checked with the airlines and they occasionally ship bodies for burial elsewhere, just like the trains do. And, though they don't like to admit it, they don't give a sealed casket the same tough security inspection they give other cargo. What I mean is, they don't generally open it as long as it looks right."

"So?"

"So Stone and his gang built their bomb in the mortuary they'd rented just for that reason—because it was a mortuary. They stuck it in a coffin—if there wasn't an old one left lying around, they're not that hard to come by—delivered it to the airport in a genuine hearse and sent it off to Rome. Not on the same flight they took, though, and that threw me for a minute. Then I asked myself: Would I like to fly nine thousand miles with a homemade bomb in the hold? So I checked the other overseas carriers. One of them shipped a body—supposedly a Vittorio Scuzzi—to Rome six hours after Stone left. That made psychological sense. Practical sense, too, because by leaving before it, they'd be ready and waiting to pick it up when it arrived."

"Are you finished?" Womack asked impatiently.

"The way I see it, General, I'm just beginning."

"Aren't you forgetting something? The case is already solved."

"Not yet, it isn't." Gamble put an insistent hand on his arm. "Can't you see that what you call a solution may be only wishful thinking? We don't have any hard-and-fast evidence that the ploot bomb was aboard the *Charles E. Moore.* All we've actually got is Neff's assumption that it was, based on another assumption: That the FALN was responsible for the hijacking."

"Jesus!" Womack groaned. "Next you'll be telling me that

the ship didn't actually blow up, either."

"Oh, it blew up, all right. But it was carrying a cargo of chemical fertilizer, nitrates, extremely explosive under the right conditions. That whole ship was a floating bomb. A bolt of lightning could have set it off."

"You're conveniently overlooking the radioactive fallout."

"Which was considerably less than it should have been. Even Neff admits that. The French exploded a nuclear device in the atmosphere ten days ago near Tahiti. If the wind was right, it would take their fallout just about that long to reach the latitude where the freighter went down."

Womack's voice had an edge to it, as though its owner was restraining his anger with considerable effort. " 'If. Maybe. Perhaps.' You fault Neff on hard-and-fast evidence . . . and you don't have a shred of it yourself. You build a half-assed theory based on nothing more than guesswork—and you expect me to swallow it."

"You don't have to swallow it yet, General. But at least don't spit it out until I've had the chance to test it."

"Meaning what?"

"Meaning I want your permission to go to Rome as I originally planned and continue the investigation there."

Womack shook his head sharply and decisively. "Permission denied."

"Why? What harm can it possibly do?"

"The matter has been officially terminated. I've advised the President to that effect. I can't go back to him now and say that I've decided to reopen it—solely on the basis of Gus Gamble's intuition."

"Then don't tell him," Gamble argued. "Don't tell anybody. Let it be our little secret."

"We've been mighty fortunate so far in keeping this thing under wraps. That's largely due to the fact that we could confine the investigation to our own backyard. But if I let you

119

go poking around Europe, it's bound to come out. Do you have any notion what the repercussions would be?"

"No. But I do have some notion what the repercussions would be if you don't let me go poking around—and Simon Stone explodes his bomb."

Womack finally lost command of his temper; had there been a desk available, he would have pounded on it. "Simon Stone is not going to explode a bomb because Simon Stone does not have a bomb to explode. The bomb—the real bomb, the only bomb!—has already exploded and the guilty parties are dead. How many times do I have to say it? The case is closed!"

"Simply saying it's closed doesn't actually close it, General."

"Then let's put it this way," Womack snapped. "My saying so closes it as far as you're concerned, mister! Tenacity used to be your virtue. Damned if you haven't turned it into a vice. You were the best once, but you're all washed up now. You told me that right in the beginning and I wouldn't believe it. All right, you've finally convinced me. Get back to your parish. I'm sorry as hell I ever took you away from it."

He spun on his heel and stalked stiffly into the restaurant, every inch the general officer. Gamble was left standing alone on the sidewalk. After a moment, he sighed. Both of his superiors, ecclesiastical and secular, had now ordered him to cease and desist. Both of them, from their separate viewpoints, had condemned him as a stubborn egotist, blinded to reality by his desire to recapture a bygone glory. Given the evidence, the rest of the world might well agree. So why could he still not accept the universal judgment?

"Maybe I'm as paranoid as Stone," he said aloud. And then he laughed. It was an expression not of humor but of defiance. "Well, it takes one to know one."

The
Stalk

HE HAD FIRST viewed Rome as a teen-ager in the company
of his parents, a sentimental pilgrimage on the part of his
father who, as a tank corps officer, had been present at the
1944 liberation. Subsequent visits were made alone, first only
for pleasure, later on business. Like many another foreigner
before him, he had fallen willing captive to the city's ambi-
ence, steeping himself in its culture, wooing its women and
relishing its idiosyncrasies, which elsewhere he would have
considered annoying. Along with the history and topogra-
phy, he had learned the language, if not fluently at least
serviceably.

Yet a decade had passed since he last set foot on Roman
soil. As with a man about to meet a former sweetheart,
Gamble wondered uneasily if he would still find her attractive. His first glimpse was not reassuring. The plane deposited him, weary and disheveled from the eleven-hour flight,
at an unfamiliar airport—Fiumicino, not Ciampino of mem-

ory—whose three-story glass terminal, functional and sterile, differed little from those to be found in a score of other countries around the world. The taxi he engaged for the twenty-five-mile journey into the city bore him through gleaming new suburbs and past forests of high rise apartments and islands of shopping centers where he remembered only open countryside. Save for the street signs, he could have fancied himself in the outskirts of Detroit or Chicago; there was even a trace of smog in the chill morning air.

But then he spied the lofty dome of St. Peter's dominating the horizon. As if an invisible dividing line had been passed, the new began to vanish and the old to take its place. The modern glass and steel towers gave way to squat structures of stone and brick and marble, few of which had been built in this century. The broad concrete river his taxi followed first narrowed, then broke into numerous tributaries, a tangle of cramped and twisting streets more suited to chariots than to automobiles. He rolled down the cab window in order to drink in the noise, the smell and, above all, the immense vitality of the city. Like a tonic, it revived his spirit and assuaged his apprehension. Rome—Eternal Rome—still lived and always would.

Always? Considering the reason for his presence here, that judgment might prove overly sanguine. Rome had survived the barbarian, from Alaric to Hitler. But no barbarian had been armed with anything remotely resembling the awesome fury of the plutonium atom with its potential not only for destroying whatever stood upon the earth but for making the earth itself uninhabitable for centuries to come. It was sobering to reflect that what kings and emperors had failed to accomplish with all their armies now, thanks to science and technology, lay well within the capabilities of one determined individual. A fragment of Byron came back to him: *And when Rome falls—the world.*

The International Atomic Energy Agency had its offices on Via Babuino, not far from the Piazza di Spagna and that tourist lodestone, the Spanish Steps. Few of the thousands who passed it each day were aware of its existence and fewer still could have defined its function. The Agency, established in 1968, was charged to monitor the manufacture and distribution of fissionable material and, if possible, to detect— through a system of inspections, inventories and surveillance —any diversion of that material into illegal channels. To that end, it maintained detachments in fifty countries. But while a police force of a sort, it unfortunately lacked true police powers. Should a violation of security occur, IAEA could merely report it and, when requested, advise. Corrective action was the sovereign responsibility of the nation in which the violation occurred. While the Agency lacked muscle, it did exert influence and Gamble hoped to avail himself of it.

In keeping with the Agency's international character, an Austrian and not an Italian was chief of the Rome bureau —although "chief" was a bit grandiose. Otto Lanz's department consisted of two full-time inspectors, neither based locally, plus a secretary and a clerk-typist. Lanz himself took the title seriously and ran an efficient operation, although by his own admission he was more politician than policeman.

Like a good politician, he popped out of his office upon being informed of Gamble's presence, his plump florid face glowing delightedly. "My good friend Gus Gamble!" he cried as he wrung his visitor's hand. It was an exaggeration; their previous acquaintance was slight and strictly professional in nature. "What a pleasure to see you again."

Gamble replied in kind and accepted Lanz's inevitable invitation to join him in coffee; the espresso machine was a fixture in every Roman office, as indispensable as the telephone. They carried the thick black liquid into Lanz's spacious quarters which overlooked a tiny courtyard. Lanz raised his cup in a toast. "To this most welcome reunion. What brings you to Rome? An Easter pilgrimage, perhaps?"

Obsessed with the hunt, he had nearly forgotten that this was, in fact, Holy Week. If this was Wednesday (he had to stop for a moment to be sure), then tomorrow was Maundy Thursday. "As a matter of fact, Otto, I'm here on business. I'm working on a case and I'm going to need a little help from you. Maybe a lot of help."

"Indeed? It was my understanding that you were no longer one of us. That you had retired several years ago."

"That's so. But I'm back now."

"In what capacity?"

Since the truth would avail him nothing, he had no recourse except to lie. "Didn't you get General Womack's letter?"

"I'm afraid not." It was hardly surprising, inasmuch as no letter had been sent, but Lanz, unaware of this, sought another explanation. "It's the postal system, of course. An absolute shambles, incredible! What should arrive in hours, arrives in weeks, even months—if, in fact, it ever arrives at all." He was venting a common annoyance, not only of foreigners but the natives as well. Someone had said that there were only two countries in the world—Tibet was the other —in which it was impossible to communicate through the mails. This was hyperbole, of course. However, it was not unusual for a letter mailed in Naples to take three weeks to reach Rome, a distance of a hundred miles—and there were verified instances where postal workers, facing a mountain of undelivered mail, had simply burned it.

Since the chaotic system worked to his benefit in this instance, Gamble did not join in complaining about it. "It'll probably be along in a day or so. In the meantime, I guess you're going to have to take me on faith."

"Certainly," Lanz agreed readily. "I will need to have

official corroboration, of course, but until I receive it, there is no reason to stand on formality. Tell me your problem and how I can help you to solve it."

Gamble obliged at length. Lanz listened with mounting agitation. "For years we have feared that such a thing might happen," he muttered. "It is the nightmare we have lived with, never really expecting that it might come true. My friend, are you positive that the device is here? Could you be mistaken?"

"Yes, I could be mistaken. But the evidence suggests that I'm not."

"But it is so incredible! To be perfectly frank, if someone else had told me this story, a man without your considerable reputation, I would dismiss it as fiction."

Welcome to the club, Gamble thought. Lanz was echoing the skepticism shared by Womack, Neff and, in fact, everyone to whom the theory had been presented, in part or in whole. And Gamble had no doubt that, were he aware of his visitor's true status, the plump Austrian would dismiss him as firmly as his American counterparts, though perhaps more politely. "I agree with you, Otto. It is incredible. But look at the world and what do you see? Maniacs hijacking planes, murdering innocent people, taking hostages, exploding bombs—for reasons which normal human beings can't comprehend. Simon Stone isn't that different from the IRA terrorists or the Palestinian guerrillas or our American Weatherman. What sets him apart is that he's got a bigger bomb."

"But those you've mentioned are political fanatics," Lanz objected.

"So is Stone in his own way. He's simply dressed his political fanaticism in religious clothes—which makes him even more dangerous."

Lanz stared out the window. It was beginning to rain, a

soft swirling mist which turned the courtyard as gloomy as his expression. "I suppose anything is possible these days," he grumbled. "What do you want me to do?"

"For openers, help me find out what happened to that casket."

Lanz rang up the airport officials at Fiumicino. Thanks to his position, he was able to secure the required information with an ease which Gamble, lacking his clout, would have been unable to duplicate. The body of Vittorio Scuzzi (or, at least, the coffin in which it presumably resided; once again, there had been no inspection) had arrived on schedule. Someone had removed it for burial, a member of the family, the officials supposed; the signature was undecipherable. The place of interment—that much was clear—was given as Amaseno, a small village midway between Rome and Naples.

Lanz found that heartening. "If, as you believe, the target is Rome, they would scarcely transport the bomb to such an out-of-the-way spot as Amaseno."

"Who says they did?" Gamble countered. "Feel like going for a drive in the country, Otto? I've got an uncontrollable urge to visit Vittorio Scuzzi's grave. If any."

The rain stopped before they reached their destination but the low clouds remained, obscuring the tops of the mountains and painting the countryside a cheerless gray. Amaseno lay several kilometers west of the autostrada, the Italian equivalent of the American freeway, with Frosinone its closest neighbor of any size. The village, nestled in a serene valley, was typical of many that could be found tucked away amid the foothills of the Apennines. Its people, by and large, were farmers. They raised wheat and maize and vegetables on the valley flatland, and vineyards flourished on the slopes.

The town itself was old, how old Gamble could only guess;

these remote villages had a way of appearing to have existed forever. Lanz informed him that Amaseno had been heavily damaged during the war, requiring extensive rebuilding. However, since everything was wrought from the same gray native stone, it was difficult to distinguish new construction from old, as though the natives were determined to retain the town's ancient character. Yet the twentieth century could be plainly seen, if not in architecture then in technology. Women still washed clothes in the spring-fed stream and donkeys still carried produce from field to market—but automobiles traveled the single street wide enough to admit them and television antennae sprouted on many rooftops. Furthermore, the younger generation had discarded the simple peasant garb for the gaudy fashions of the city, a strong indication that Amaseno's traditional way of life was passing.

Lanz suggested they seek out Amaseno's mayor. Gamble chose to consult its priest instead, reasoning that in these small villages the clergy was generally better informed on matters of life and death (burial certainly came under that heading) than the politicians.

The church, named in honor of Saint Lorenzo, was located only a few paces off the central piazza. The small high-vaulted sanctuary was not in use at this hour of the day but the parish priest was straightening the wooden benches which served as pews in preparation for the evening Mass. Father Giorgio was a sallow-faced young man, recently ordained, who took his responsibilities seriously. His accent indicated that he came from the north of Italy.

Gamble allowed Lanz to do the talking; he feared that his own accent might prove a hindrance. Lanz, ever the diplomat, took his time, praising the church and inquiring into its history, before tackling the matter which had brought them to it. Even then, he did so obliquely. "We are not, as you are aware, of Amaseno. However, I hope that you will consent to do us a service regardless. We have been told, perhaps inaccurately, that another stranger, one Vittorio Scuzzi, was recently buried here."

Gamble expected a blank look. To his surprise, Father Giorgio nodded. "Yes, that is correct."

"Are you certain about that, Father? Vittorio Scuzzi? From America?"

Another nod. "Signor Scuzzi was laid to rest only two days ago. Even if it had not been so recent, I would have remembered it because of the unusual circumstances."

"Unusual in what way?" Gamble asked, abandoning his bystander role.

"Unusual in that there are no Scuzzis in Amaseno. I was informed that Vittorio lived here as a child and expressed a desire to be buried here. No one I've talked with remembers him."

"Who informed you of all this, Father? Not Vittorio, certainly."

No, there had been a letter accompanying the casket which had arrived from Rome by truck; Father Giorgio named a large delivery company. He had retained the letter "somewhere" and offered to seek it out. Gamble declined. He felt sure he would learn nothing from it, or from the delivery company, either. He had come to respect the enemy's talent for covering his tracks.

His frown made the priest uneasy. "I hope, signore, that you don't feel I've committed an impropriety. Everything was done in the manner prescribed."

"If we seem distraught, Father, it's simply that we regret arriving too late for the funeral. Would it be permissible for us to view the grave?"

Amaseno's cemetery lay some distance from the town, atop a hillock on the opposite side of the valley, as if to mark

128

a geographical as well as a physical distinction between the living and the dead. It was, in fact, not a cemetery at all but a mausoleum, open to the sky and surrounded by a tall stone wall. A few trees shaded it but there was no grass and no flowers; the earth was carpeted with gravel. Inside was a maze composed of shorter but much thicker walls, death's filing cabinet, in which the bodies were lodged. Many of the concrete alcoves were empty, patiently awaiting the eventual arrival of their occupants. Marble headstones, some inset with photographs, both hid and identified those already in residence here, their elaborateness varying with the affluence of the survivors.

Entrance to the mausoleum was through a double gate of grilled iron which could be locked, though for what purpose it was difficult to determine—since who would wish to break into a graveyard? The gate was open when Gamble and Lanz arrived and a man, carrying a mortar-encrusted bucket and a trowel, was just leaving.

"Vittorio Scuzzi? I have only this moment finished setting his headstone. Turn left, then right." The stonemason departed, whistling. It was simply a job to him and carried with it no particular solemnity.

The mausoleum appeared to be arranged by families of which Amaseno, like most small villages, did not have a great many. Vittorio Scuzzi, who belonged to none of them, had been placed somewhat apart with no immediate neighbors to keep him company. His marker also was functional rather than decorative, containing only his name and two dates; there was no photograph.

"Well?" Lanz demanded, shivering, more in reaction to the rain which was beginning to fall again than from the morbid surroundings. "You asked to see a grave—and here it is. Are you satisfied?"

"The mortar's still soft, luckily," Gamble observed, testing the joint with his finger.

"You're surely not suggesting that we open it?"

"It's high time somebody looked inside the casket."

"But that's illegal—or, at the very least, sacrilegious!"

"Don't worry. I happen to be a priest myself." Lanz assumed he was joking; Gamble made no effort to persuade him otherwise. "If you have qualms, Otto, why don't you wait for me in the car?"

Qualms Lanz undoubtedly had, but his sense of duty overrode them. He watched uneasily as Gamble dug away the fresh mortar with his pocketknife. "I hope you have a good excuse ready in case we're caught."

Gamble smiled thinly. "I'll plead insanity."

"That may well be true," Lanz muttered. "But I'm not sure that it constitutes a defense. Can't you work a little faster?"

With the mortar removed, Gamble was able to get the knife blade behind the marble slab and lever it free. In the exposed crypt, and nearly filling it, reposed a bronze coffin which, in both shape and color, resembled a large freshly baked loaf of bread. "Give me a hand, Otto."

Lanz obeyed reluctantly. Together they wrestled the casket from its resting place, nearly dropping it in the process, and lowered it to the gravel. "It's certainly heavy enough to contain a body," Lanz ventured as though hoping that this might end the matter.

Gamble had not come this far to stop now. "We'll know in a minute." The rounded lid was hinged on one side and secured by hasps on the other. He flung open the lid. There was a moment of silence, broken only by the murmur of the rain.

"Empty!" Lanz whispered, his surprise evidence of how little faith he had placed in Gamble's story. No corpse reposed on the quilted satin lining. In its place the bronze box

130

carried a far different—and less grisly—burden. "Rocks. Nothing but a lot of rocks."

"Rocks? Not exactly. Don't you see, Otto? It's a joke. A very private joke that no one was ever meant to know." Gamble closed the casket lid slowly. "I think that if you'd ask the chap who put them there, he'd tell you that they're —stones."

"There's a man I think you should meet," Lanz said as they drove back to Rome. Behind them they left a crypt to which the bogus coffin had been returned and its misleading marker restored, although the latter was now held in place by mud rather than mortar. "His name is Fuselli and he is a police officer. Not yet the top man in his department—but I've found that, when I need a thing to be done and done quickly, Ugo is the person to see." He hesitated. "However, I should warn you that he is a Communist."

He assumed that Gamble, as an American, might be disturbed by the fact. "As long as Fuselli's a good cop, I don't much care what else he is." The Italian Communist party was Western Europe's largest but its members were, by and large, nationalists who owed little or no allegiance to their Soviet counterpart. In any case, the present danger transcended politics; he was willing to take allies where he found them.

Lanz drove directly to police headquarters—although "directly" was a misleading description of the route forced upon them by the confusing tangle of one-way streets through which the late afternoon traffic raced (not infrequently in the wrong direction) with a magnificent disregard for life and limb. Lanz, who handled his little Fiat with the aplomb of a native, explained that the secret was to appear never to be aware of the other drivers. "If you so much as glance in their direction, they take it as an invitation to dominate you, to

131

crowd you out." This gladiatorial philosophy—to which even the pedestrians subscribed—appeared to work: There were fewer serious accidents here than in any American city of comparable size. However, the wear and tear on the nerves was another matter.

Despite Gamble's apprehension, they reached their destination safely, only to learn that the journey was in vain. The deputy chief, Special Operations Section, was not in his office. His secretary informed them that Colonel Fuselli was suffering from a chill and had gone home early.

"A common complaint, particularly on dull afternoons," Lanz told Gamble with a wink. "And one for which bed rest is the only cure. Let's hope that Ugo chose to recuperate in his own bed."

He had. Lanz reached him by telephone at home and, following a guarded conversation, informed Gamble that they had been invited to supper that evening. "It's better this way. By meeting unofficially, it permits us to keep the matter off the record until we choose to put it there."

"You're still not completely convinced, are you, Otto?"

"Let us say that I continue to hope you are mistaken." Lanz shrugged. "But I scarcely matter. Your job is to convince Fuselli."

Ugo Fuselli might be a Communist, but he lived like a capitalist. His home was a spacious condominium apartment in Cinecittà, a relatively new suburb which—as the name indicated—was the citadel of the Italian film industry. He resided there with his wife, a blonde beauty from Puglia on Italy's Adriatic coast, their two small but well-mannered children and a widowed aunt. Fuselli was in his forties, a slender man with the saturnine aristocratic features of a Renaissance prince. It was a face which, although it wore a smile much of the time, concealed more than it revealed; Gamble suspected that his temper was as quick as his wit.

132

Supper was an exclusively male affair, an indication that business rather than pleasure was its raison d'être. It began with a thick lentil soup and a Positano salad—tomatoes and provolone cheese—and the inevitable pasta, followed by veal and stuffed zucchini, all accompanied by a full-bodied vino rosso from the Castelli Romano vineyards. Chilled melon and coffee, a rich cappuccino, completed the feast.

Fuselli was a charming host, keeping the conversation flowing as readily as the wine. He regaled his guests with talk of sports and politics, the latest gossip and the newest anecdote. Nothing in his easy manner suggested that his hospitality had the slightest connection with his official duties. Yet through it all his deep-set eyes studied the American without appearing to do so, weighing him impartially on the scales of experience, the sure sign of the professional policeman.

And when the table had been cleared and cigars offered, he at last permitted the policeman to emerge. "Now, Signor Gamble, I believe that you have a matter of some consequence you wish to present to me."

He listened to the story in silence, eyes fixed intently on Gamble's face, his own expression inscrutable. "Very interesting," he murmured.

Gamble sighed; the noncommittal reaction was depressingly familiar. "But, of course, you don't believe a word of it."

"Have I said that I don't?" Fuselli replied mildly.

"No. But you haven't said that you do, either."

"To be honest with you, Signor Gamble, I find your story of a plot against the Vatican melodramatic to say the least. But that's no reason to reject it out of hand. Each day I become more convinced that I am surrounded by madmen."

"Present company excepted, I hope."

"At the same time," Fuselli continued, "I must judge on the evidence you have presented. Please don't be offended if

I say that it does not completely convince me."

"Maybe I didn't tell it very well."

"On the contrary. It's simply that . . . Let me illustrate." He collected his guests' empty wine glasses and ranged them on the table before him. "Here we have the man, Simon Stone. Here, the stolen plutonium, call it the bomb, if you will. And here, the coffin you opened at Amaseno. Each exists, that no one can deny. But are the three necessarily connected?"

Gamble placed two of the goblets in the center of the table. "Here's something else no one can deny. Both Simon Stone and the coffin arrived in Rome from Los Angeles at virtually the same time. Isn't it reasonable to suppose that the bomb" —he picked up the third glass—"came with them?"

"Only if you accept as fact what is still merely supposition. Did Stone and his gang of thugs steal the plutonium? Is the Pope their target? Did they use the coffin to transport a bomb? To each of these questions, your answer is a resounding yes! My own answer, however, is only—perhaps."

"That should be enough," Gamble argued. "As long as there's even the barest possibility that I may be right, you can't afford to ignore it. You've got to find Simon Stone and make sure. And you've got to find him fast."

"Are you aware that Rome's population numbers over three million? And at this time of year—Holy Week—we play host to perhaps a hundred thousand visitors and tourists, besides. To expect that I can simply reach out my hand and seize one individual among millions, especially an individual who may not wish to be found—"

"Stone's a foreigner. That should make it harder for him to hide."

"Italy has no registration requirement. The problem is the same, no matter what the man's nationality."

"I'm disappointed, Colonel." He had come nine thousand

miles only to encounter once again the same official lethargy he had left behind and he couldn't keep anger out of his voice. "Anyone can furnish a dozen reasons why the difficult is impossible. Otto bragged that you were the one man in Rome who could be counted on to get things done. But perhaps Otto exaggerated."

Lanz stirred uneasily but Fuselli remained unperturbed. "How would you have me vindicate my reputation?" he inquired. "Should I request the government to proclaim a state of emergency?"

"If there's no other way, yes."

"Even if I believe that the government would listen to me —which I don't—I wouldn't make the request. My responsibility is to guard the public safety against those who would endanger it. By the same token, it is also my responsibility not to do anything myself which will endanger it."

"I'm not suggesting that you should."

"Aren't you? Consider the consequences of overreacting. Panic, riots, a mass exodus, the utter collapse of society. I shudder to estimate how many would die trying to flee the city in order to 'save' themselves. And from what? A bomb which may not even exist—or which, if it does exist, may not be within ten thousand kilometers of Rome."

"In other words, you'd let the boat sink rather than take a chance of alarming the passengers."

"But is the boat actually sinking? Or do you merely imagine that it is?"

"I don't know!" Gamble said, his voice rising. "Ask me again when we're all drowning!"

"Gus, calm down," Lanz interposed nervously. "There's no need to shout."

Gamble knew that he was behaving boorishly but he was too weary to care. Jet lag, assisted by too much food and too much wine, was taking its toll. His circadian clock was still

135

set on California time and it told him that it was actually five o'clock in the morning. "What's the use?" he muttered. He put his hands on the table and used them to push his body erect. "Thanks for the dinner, at least."

"Sit down," Fuselli requested. "We haven't finished."

"I think we have, Colonel. I've got work to do and not much time to do it. Simon Stone's out there someplace. Maybe I can find him and maybe I can't—but I'm not going to sit here and argue about it any longer."

"Sit down," Fuselli repeated and this time it was an order. "Your manner is offensive but I'll be charitable and put it down to fatigue. At the risk of being equally offensive, let me confess that I would be pleased never to see you again." He shrugged. "But I suppose that I will simply have to make the best of it."

Gamble stared at him, his brain too numbed to grasp the significance of the words. "I am going to help you," Fuselli explained gently. "I still don't entirely believe that we are teetering on the edge of doom. But I am impressed by the fact that you believe it with such passion. Because of that I will present this matter to my superiors for exactly what it is." He held up a cautioning finger. "An unsubstantiated theory, possibly no more than a figment of the imagination . . . along with the request that I be allowed to conduct a thorough investigation of it."

"Thank you," Gamble whispered. He sat down and was surprised to find that he was trembling. For a moment he feared he might burst into tears. "You won't regret it."

"That remains to be seen." Fuselli rose and held out his hand. "Good night, signor. Go back to your hotel. Sleep. In the morning, we will begin."

Most men would have accepted that as victory. Gamble could not resist reaching for more. "Why can't you get started on it tonight?"

Fuselli's eyebrows shot up. "Disturb the commissioner at this hour? Do you have any notion what he . . ." He saw Gamble's jaw set stubbornly and he threw up his hands in surrender. "All right—I'll risk it rather than endure another argument." He laughed helplessly. "You promised me that I would have no regrets. My friend, I already have them!"

Gamble had neglected to book lodgings in advance. Even if it had occurred to him to do so, the effort would have been futile. Rome was awash with visitors. The tourist hotels were crammed to capacity and had been for days with pilgrims drawn from near and far for the celebration of Holy Week.

However, Otto Lanz—who had lived in Rome almost long enough to consider himself a native—used a combination of cajolery and bribery to obtain a room in a small pensione on Via del Corso, Rome's Broadway. Although the pensione lacked many of the luxuries which Americans consider necessities, the room was clean and the bed comfortable. Not that the latter really mattered; in his immense fatigue, Gamble would have accepted a concrete slab without complaint.

It was nearly noon when he awoke. Sleep had not refreshed him as he had hoped it would. Instead, he felt somewhat depressed and disoriented. Yesterday's crowded appointment pad and its disparate cast of characters—Lanz, Father Giorgio, Fuselli, the mythical Vittorio Scuzzi—now seemed more a dream than a reality. He was troubled by a feeling that he should be doing something if only he could remember what that something was.

Had Fuselli attempted to contact him? He dressed hurriedly and went downstairs. The portiere—who owned the only telephone in the pensione—was an elderly arthritic who could be forgiven for declining to climb the stairs to deliver a message to his sleeping guest. However, no forgiveness was necessary. Fuselli had not called.

Prudence dictated that he return to his room and wait. But who could say how long that might be? The prospect of being cooped up like a prisoner while every fiber of his being demanded action was intolerable. Even prisoners were permitted exercise. He informed the portiere that he was going for a short walk.

Yesterday's rain had vanished and sunshine had replaced it. It was a day conducive to strolling. Although winter was still in residence, there was the promise of spring in the crisp air. In this, the core of the city, automobiles were barred during the midday hours and the narrow streets held only pedestrians, many of them tourists armed with guidebooks and cameras. The visitors trudged this way and that with what seemed to be a cheerless determination to leave none of the famous monuments unviewed and unphotographed.

Gamble followed their example. He nourished a vague hope that the familiar landmarks, reassuring in their timelessness, would lift his spirits. It was too much to expect of stone and marble. The Piazza del Pópolo with its famed Egyptian obelisk was cluttered with tour buses, causing it to resemble a parking lot. On the Spanish Steps, the flower vendors of the past were gone and the flower children of the present—*i capelloni* in Roman parlance, the long-haired ones—had taken their place, eking out their counter-culture existence by hawking bad art and cheap jewelry. The famed Trevi Fountain, that baroque fantasy of gods, goddesses, tritons and sea horses, had been drained in order to clean it. Since the work had not yet begun, the algae-crusted basin gave off a distinctly unpleasant odor.

He became aware that someone else was following the same aimless itinerary. She was in her twenties, a slender woman with taffy-colored hair and an impudently pretty face with a generous mouth and high cheekbones which gave her violet eyes a slightly oriental cast. She wore no makeup or jewelry and her costume, slacks and a pullover sweater, did little to emphasize her femininity. Despite this, there was something inherently sensual about her, the sort of woman men will instinctively glance at twice without really knowing why.

She noticed his covert scrutiny and rewarded it with a smile, then surprised him by speaking to him in throaty English. "I wonder if it still works when it's empty."

"What?"

"Haven't you heard the legend? That if you throw a coin into the Trevi Fountain, you'll surely come back to Rome?"

"Yes, I've heard that." Her English, though good, was not her native tongue, but neither the slight accent nor her appearance told Gamble what her true nationality might be. "But I don't know whether the water makes any difference."

"Well, there's no harm in trying." She fumbled in her purse. "Oh, dear! I've nothing but paper."

"Be my guest," Gamble said, offering her a 100-lire-piece. He wondered if it might not be a new method of panhandling.

It wasn't, because she asked, "You've nothing smaller?"

"As a matter of fact, it's the only coin I do have."

"In that case, perhaps it will do for both of us." She closed her eyes and tossed the coin over her shoulder in the prescribed fashion. It clattered on the marble basin and bounced into a stagnant puddle. "There! And now tell me—how may I return the favor?"

The proper next move was to invite her to have coffee, even —considering the hour—lunch. Gamble felt sure that should he do so, she would not refuse it or, perhaps, a later and more serious proposal. He could not deny that he was tempted. The beguiling woman, the sensual city—or a combination of both—aroused a desire he had nearly forgotten. He thrust it aside with an effort. As a priest, he could not succumb to it;

139

as a policeman, he should not. In neither role was he free to pursue personal pleasure. However, the fact that she was forbidden fruit made her no less attractive. "Don't mention it," he said awkwardly. "It was only a hundred lire."

The young woman studied him as if she were able to read his thoughts and was secretly amused by them. "Well, thanks, anyway. Perhaps we'll run into each other again—on our next visit." She gave him another smile and sauntered away, a lithe young animal, graceful in every movement.

He returned slowly to the pensione. The walk had done nothing to refresh him—but the message which awaited him did. Fuselli had phoned in his absence. Failing to find him in, he had left word for Gamble to meet him at the IAEA office immediately.

The Agency, in keeping with Roman custom, was closed between the hours of one and four. The secretary and clerk-typist were gone; Otto Lanz unlocked the door to admit him. Both his face and his greeting were abnormally grim. He ushered Gamble into the inner office where Fuselli was sitting, an unlit cigar clamped between his teeth.

"Sorry to keep you waiting," Gamble apologized, short of breath more from anticipation than exertion. "What's happened?"

Fuselli replied without removing the cigar. "I wish to inform you that I have found your Simon Stone."

"That's marvelous! Fantastic! How did you do it so quickly?"

"It wasn't as difficult as I anticipated." Oddly enough, the fact seemed to give him no satisfaction. "You mentioned that Stone had come to Rome on the pretense of seeking medical treatment. I set my men checking all the hospitals and nursing homes. Stone is a patient at the Santa Maria Hospital."

"Then what are we waiting for? Let's go get him."

"I think not," Fuselli said softly. With sudden anger, he

140

flung the dead cigar in the general direction of the wastebasket. "The comedy is over."

"What are you talking about?"

Lanz said, "Gus, I spoke to General Womack this morning." He added unnecessarily, "By telephone."

Gamble's mouth was suddenly dry. "Oh," he said; nothing better came to mind.

"I believe you can guess what the General told me," Lanz continued in a reproachful voice. "You have no authority here—or anywhere. You were ordered not to come, in fact. As if that were not enough, the bomb has already been exploded and the missing plutonium accounted for. Everything you told us yesterday was a fiction."

"No." Gamble shook his head. "I'll admit that I didn't level with you regarding my own status. I'm sorry about that —but it was the only way I could get you to listen to me."

"You made a fool of me," Fuselli accused. "I accepted you as a man of honor, only to discover that you have no honor."

"Maybe that's true but it's not important. The only important thing is that you follow up on Simon Stone and—"

"Mother of God! You lie to me, you set my whole department on a wild-goose chase, you embarrass me with my superiors and still you expect . . . You must be mad!"

"Last night you said you were impressed by the strength of my conviction. It's as strong as ever, Colonel. I'm absolutely convinced that Stone has to be found and stopped before it's too late."

"Your own government tells us that the case is closed and that Simon Stone is innocent. But that means nothing, of course. They are wrong and you are right. Never mind that all the evidence is on the other side—"

"Not quite all. How about that empty coffin at Amaseno?"

"As I pointed out to you last evening, there is no established connection between the coffin and Simon Stone. The coffin may have been used by someone to smuggle something into Italy. But that someone was not Stone and that something was not a bomb."

"What sort of a cop are you?" Gamble demanded, desperation in his voice. "You can't be sure of that. You've got to check it out!"

Fuselli's expression was uncompromising. "I'm through playing games, Signor. And so are you."

Lanz said, "General Womack urged that you should be deported. I've persuaded Ugo to spare us all that embarrassment. I'm sure you'll be leaving Italy in any case." While he might be as offended as Fuselli by Gamble's deceit, his politician's instinct was to conciliate.

Gamble rejected it. "Go ahead and arrest me. Maybe the publicity will help me get a little action."

Fuselli sprang up. "Let us understand each other," he growled. "I'm willing to overlook the trouble you've caused me. But I'm not willing to allow you to create panic with your vicious rumors. You remain in Rome only on the condition that you drop this insanity, immediately and completely. Otherwise, I'll have you on an airplane within an hour— under guard and in a muzzle if necessary. Which is it going to be, my friend?"

Further defiance was tempting but it would be profitless. Deported, he could do nothing; only by remaining in the game could he hope to influence the outcome. It was an exceedingly faint hope—but it was all he had. "Have it your way, Colonel. I'll stay and I'll behave myself." He laughed bitterly. "You called me crazy. Well, considering that I know what's coming and still don't get the hell out of here, I guess I must be."

Fuselli had also called him a liar. That accusation, at least, was valid. Despite his promise, Gamble had no intention of

142

behaving himself. He was surprised that Fuselli had accepted his word so readily. Or had he? As he returned to the pensione, Gamble glanced over his shoulder, frequently but casually, to see if he was being followed. He couldn't detect anyone among his fellow pedestrians who looked like a cop. But to be on the safe side, when he rounded the next corner he stepped into a convenient doorway and waited.

"What in the world are you doing?" a voice inquired. It was the young woman from the Trevi Fountain. She stood on the opposite sidewalk, sipping a Coca-Cola and regarding him curiously.

"Oh, I just stopped to catch my breath." The explanation didn't make much sense but it was better than nothing.

She strolled across the street to join him. "It looked to me like you were hiding from someone."

"Why would I do that?" he parried.

She shrugged. "I don't know. That's just the way it looked."

"To tell you the truth," Gamble said, feigning sheepishness, "I'm lost. I've been hunting for a cab to take me back to my hotel."

"You won't find a cab around here at this hour. You'll have to leave the restricted area. Piazza Barberini is probably the closest. Go east three blocks, then turn south . . ." She hesitated. "Perhaps I'd better show you. I'm going that way myself."

Having professed that he was lost, Gamble could scarcely turn down the offer of a guide. For that matter, he didn't really want to. Hers was the only friendly face he'd seen all day; not only that, it was an extremely attractive face. Once again he found himself responding to the aura of sensuality she wore like a perfume. Yet she exhibited no coquetry, made no pretty pretense of feminine dependency. She did not take his arm but walked with a jaunty independence, easily matching his stride. If their shoulders occasionally brushed, it was by accident and not design.

"You seem to know your way around pretty well for a tourist," he observed.

"Oh, I'm not really a tourist. I'm studying at the University."

"Then what was all that about tossing a coin into the fountain?"

"I'd never done it before," she explained, then gave him a puckish smile. "Good heavens! Did you think I was a *ragazza squillo,* a—what is the phrase?—a call girl?"

"Certainly not," he lied. "I assumed you were just being friendly."

She laughed. "Men often consider it the same thing. But you're right. It's such a beautiful day—and yet you looked so grim, as though you were carrying the weight of the world on your shoulders. I thought a smile might help."

"As you can see, it worked wonders."

"I see nothing of the sort," she told him candidly. "You seem even gloomier than before."

Her perception was disturbing. He had always prided himself on an ability to mask his feelings. Had he lost that, too? "I'm worried about business," he alibied. "A deal that isn't turning out the way I hoped."

"I'm sorry." She put a compassionate hand on his arm. "Would you feel better if you talked about it? I know nothing about business—but I'm a splendid listener."

Her offer of a sympathetic ear (or a shoulder to cry on) was appealing. But his burden could not—and should not—be shared with a stranger, however charming. "That's very nice of you but I'm on my way to an important meeting."

"Oh? I thought you said you were returning to your hotel."

One lie leads to another. "The meeting's at my hotel."

144

Her interest in his troubles, casual at best, evaporated. "Well, I hope it's successful. Ah, there's your taxi." They had reached Piazza Barberini, the noisy intersection of a half dozen streets, including the famed Via Veneto, through which the traffic flowed in a circular pattern like a never-ceasing carousel.

She waved her arms to attract the attention of the cruising taxi, then ran with him to it when the vehicle stopped. "Which hotel?" she asked Gamble, apparently assuming that he spoke no Italian.

He supplied the first name that came to mind. "The Hilton."

She relayed the information to the driver and turned away with a wave, her responsibility fulfilled. "Hey, wait a minute," he called. He didn't even know her name; realistically, she was of no more significance than anyone else in the city's three million population. But she had been kind to him and she was lovely and he couldn't allow her to become just a statistic. "Do you have friends in Italy? Outside of Rome, I mean."

"Yes." Her expression was puzzled. "Why do you ask?"

"Go visit them," he urged. "Get out of the city. Today. I can't tell you why—but trust me. It might save your life."

She stared at him. "Are you serious?"

"You'd better believe it. Somebody better." The taxi lurched off. When he looked back, she was already lost from sight. He would never see her again and thus would never know if she had heeded his advice. The odds were that she would not; no one else had. Well, he had done his best. The way things were going that might have to serve as his epitaph.

He tapped the driver on the shoulder. "Forget the Hilton. I want to go to the Santa Maria Hospital instead."

The driver regarded him curiously. "Are you ill, signor?"

"Maybe. I won't know for sure until I've been to the hospital."

L'Ospedale di Santa Maria was situated not far from the Baths of Caracalla and closer still to an even more ancient ruin, the massive wall which had encircled the city in pre-Christian times. The hospital was not among Rome's largest or most prestigious; from the street, it resembled an exclusive hotel. The main building, in fact, had once been a private villa and was probably a century old. A second building, attached to the first and nearly hidden behind it, had been added within the past decade with no attempt to duplicate the baroque architecture of the original. The juxtaposition of the old and the new was not remarkable. Rome was a city which preserved its past while making no pretense of living in it.

Stone pillars flanked an entrance designed for carriages. Beyond them the drive curved up a slight hill to the broad marble steps of the former villa. Gamble would not have been surprised if a footman had bounded out to greet him. He paid the driver and went inside.

The high-ceilinged foyer was empty, save for an old woman dressed in black who was mopping the terrazzo floor. The day's incoming patients had checked in earlier; those departing had already gone and visiting hours were still some time off. There was no one behind the admissions counter. Gamble rang the bell and waited.

After a while, a ferret-faced young man appeared, struggling to put on his white jacket and smooth down his black hair simultaneously. He had the air of one who has been interrupted at some important task but his sleepy eyes suggested otherwise. "Bruno Caccavale at your service, signor."

"I'd like to inquire about one of your patients."

"Member of the family?" the young man inquired, stifling a yawn.

"An old friend."

"We're not allowed to discuss the condition of our patients." He said it with some satisfaction as if to repay the visitor for having awakened him. "You'll have to speak to the doctor."

"Actually, I'm only trying to make sure that my friend is here. You can tell me that, can't you?"

"I suppose so," Caccavale admitted reluctantly. "What is your friend's name?" Gamble told him. He repeated it, frowning; then his expression lightened. "Ah, yes! The American gentleman from California."

"That's the one. Would you mind telling me his room number? I'd like to drop in on him." Anticipating an objection, he added, "During visiting hours, of course."

Caccavale shook his head, anyway. "I'm afraid that's impossible."

"You mean he's too sick to have visitors."

"I mean that Signor Stone has no room here. He is an outpatient. He comes to our clinic only for treatment."

"Naturally," Gamble murmured. Simon Stone would not wish to confine himself to the strict routine of a hospital. As an outpatient he could come and go as he pleased, while still using his illness as camouflage. "In that case, can you tell me where he's staying?"

"I don't have that information, signor."

"It must be in your records," Gamble persisted. Every hospital in the world required the patient to list an address, if only to know where to send the bill.

"Perhaps," Caccavale agreed. "But the records are not here and, in any case, they are confidential. If you wish to

147

leave a message, I'll see that your friend receives it on his next visit."

Since that would not serve his purpose, Gamble adopted a coaxing tone. "Can't I persuade you to bend the rule a little in this case? Simon doesn't know I'm in Rome. I'd like to surprise him."

The young man regarded him narrowly. "You don't realize what you're asking. Perhaps your friend will not appreciate being surprised. One never knows. If he should complain, I might lose my job."

His words carried finality but his tone did not. Neither did he turn away from the counter to indicate that the matter was closed. Instead, he waited, his expression expectant. Gamble recognized it for what it was, an invitation to bargain. He placed a 10,000-lire note on the counter.

Caccavale didn't acknowledge its presence. "I would like to accommodate you, signor. But a man must also look out for himself."

Gamble put another note on top of the first. Caccavale's eyes flickered, a sure indication to the experienced blackjack dealer that he was tempted. But still he hesitated, wondering if he might drive up the price farther. Gamble made up his mind for him. "Perhaps you're right," he said with a shrug. "It was just a whim." He let his fingers move slowly toward the currency.

Caccavale's fingers were faster; the bills disappeared into his pocket. "Come back at six o'clock and I'll have the information for you. The files are locked at this hour."

Gamble didn't know whether to believe the facile explanation. On the other hand, he could conceive of no logical reason why the clerk would lie. Having accepted the bribe, he had placed himself at Gamble's mercy. "Okay," he said reluctantly. "Six o'clock then. I'll be back."

Caccavale caught his arm. "Please be discreet. In the evening there will be others around. Naturally, I would not want them to know of our"—he cleared his throat—"arrangement."

"In that case, why don't you telephone me? It'll save me the trip and you the embarrassment. I'm staying at the Pensione Danesi and my name is Gamble."

Caccavale wrote it down. "You will hear from me."

"One thing more. If Signor Stone should come to the hospital between now and then, you're not to mention me."

"I understand," the young man agreed slyly. "You wish to be sure that he is properly surprised."

"Only because I know what pleasure it will give him." Gamble smiled sweetly. "After all, what else are friends for?"

The Snare

THE PENSIONE DANESI provided two meals per day, one of which was supper. The menu could not be considered gourmet by any stretch of the imagination. Signora Danesi was from Salerno and cooked in the Neapolitan fashion with an emphasis on pasta. If the quality left something to be desired, the quantity did not. Neither did the warm hospitality of the cook who fretted at Gamble's lack of appetite and was greatly distressed when a mere telephone call—and not even from a woman but another man, per Dio!—caused him to abandon his half-full plate.

"I have to meet an old friend," Gamble aplogized. "Could you tell me where Via Mugnaio is?"

She could not but her husband could. And with obvious repugnance. "Surely, you're not going there at this hour of the evening?"

"Why not?"

"It is Trastevere," the old man replied simply as if that

explained everything. "Could there be some mistake? Are you certain that your friend is staying in Trastevere?"

"My friend has peculiar tastes. Would you mind calling a taxi for me?"

Trastevere is the southwestern section of Rome, a part of the old city and yet set apart from it; as the name suggests, it lies across the Tiber. More slum than suburb, it is not an area beloved by tourists. Aside from the flea market (where, it is widely believed, anything stolen the night before can be found on the morning after), there is little to attract them and Trastevere's reputation is unsavory. By day, it is a confusing tangle of streets, many no wider than alleys, noisy and noxious, a warren of shabby tenements and small shops. By night, Trastevere becomes a jungle, unlighted and ominous. The shops and trattorias, the small family restaurants, close early and there is little pedestrian traffic after dark. Like most jungles, its dangers are exaggerated—but it is also true that Trastevere harbors its share of predators waiting to pounce upon the unwary.

Gamble's driver, like the Danesis, considered his fare imprudent at best to venture into the jungle. He at least had no intention of penetrating its heart. He insisted on dropping Gamble on the comparatively secure Viale di Trastevere, several blocks from his destination, and appeared relieved that he was not asked to wait.

Trastevere was dark but by no means quiet. Music and laughter, the sound of voices raised in song or in argument, spilled out of the shuttered windows. Unseen doors slammed, dogs barked peevishly and somewhere a baby bawled. Neither was the jungle as devoid of observable life as it first appeared. In one shadowy doorway, two lovers stood embracing. In another, a group of boys, the oldest no more than ten, puffed on a scavenged cigarette while they played the finger game called morra. Once he had to step

151

aside for a large family marching home from some outing and again to avoid a helmeted young woman on a motor scooter who roared past him, exhaust popping. None paid any attention to the stranger any more than did the army of scrawny cats which prowled among the cobblestones investigating the garbage thrown from second-floor balconies.

After a while, he found Via Mugnaio, no small accomplishment in an area where few signs were posted and where the streets themselves might bear three different names in as many blocks. Mugnaio was narrower than most. By stretching out his arms, Gamble could nearly touch the buildings on either side. And it was, if possible, even darker, a roofless tunnel with no patch of light to mark the far end.

As his eyes became accustomed to the greater gloom, he could make out doorways. They gave access to inner courtyards and, beyond these, to apartments since there were no street level windows. He stopped at each, nearly pressing his nose against the stout wooden barriers like a sniffing hound in order to make out the number. They appeared to follow no logical sequence as if they had been chosen by whim or to indicate the order in which the buildings had been constructed. He could only hope that 79—the address Caccavale had given him—was not among those which bore no number at all.

Midway down the tiny street (next to number 31 and across from number 10), he found the doorway he sought. Gamble traced the numerals with an exultant finger. There was no bell and he would not have dared ring it, anyway. He tested the latch cautiously.

He sensed rather than heard a movement behind him. A thin cord bit into his throat and he was jerked off balance, falling to his knees. He sought to struggle free, to regain his feet. But there was a knee in his back now, a fulcrum against which the cord drew his body backward in an unnatural arc.

152

His frantic fingers, unable to reach his unseen assailant, strove vainly against the noose, seeking to relieve the awful pressure.

He tried to scream and could not. His lungs were threatening to burst and his eyes felt ready to pop from their sockets. His strength was going, his consciousness slipping away and he knew that his life would follow shortly. He was dying, here on the cobblestones of Trastevere, with no one to save him. Flopping about like a fish on an unbreakable line, he could only await the ultimate darkness and, with it, the end of pain.

He heard, from what seemed a great distance off, a faint popping sound. He imagined it was his neck snapping. The sound came again—and suddenly the noose released its dreadful grip. He pitched forward like a rag doll to the pavement. He lay there, inexplicably free and gloriously alive, sucking in great greedy mouthfuls of the air he had never expected to breathe again.

Something touched the back of his neck. Terror returned in a rush. He had not escaped, after all. The stranger had merely been toying with him and now meant to finish the job. Then he realized that what he felt was not the deadly rope but a soft hand. A voice in his ear—he thought it was familiar but could not place it—said, "It's all right. There's nothing to be afraid of now."

With an immense effort, he managed to turn his head. A slender figure knelt beside him, a young woman who wore a one-piece jumpsuit and a white crash helmet. She had passed him earlier on a motor scooter. Blessed chance had brought this stranger to Via Mugnaio. It was the noise of her scooter's exhaust which had frightened off his attacker. Then, as his vision commenced to clear, he saw that he was mistaken on all counts. Choice, not chance, was responsible for her presence and the popping sounds had come from the pistol she held loosely in her free hand. For that matter, she wasn't even a stranger.

"Feeling better?" she asked, stroking his head like a mother comforting a child who has had a nightmare.

"I guess so." He didn't recognize the sound of his own voice. The noose had bruised his larynx, making it painful to speak. "What are you doing here?"

"Following you," she said matter-of-factly. "I nearly lost you in the traffic coming across the bridge. A good thing I didn't."

Their encounter at the Trevi Fountain had been no accident, after all. Neither, he realized, had their second meeting. He groped for an explanation that made sense. "Are you one of Fuselli's people?"

"Hardly," she replied with a chuckle and got to her feet. "Do you mind if we discuss it later? I don't think he'll be coming back—but there's no sense taking chances."

Reminded of the danger, Gamble looked around sharply; that hurt, too. "Where did he go?"

She pointed with the pistol. "He ran off in that direction."

"Who was he? What did he look like?"

"I don't know. It was too dark. A big man, that's about all I can say. I think my second shot may have wounded him. I had to fire the first one in the air. I was afraid I might hit you."

"Was he following me, too?"

"No, I believe he was hiding in that doorway over there. I didn't see him until he jumped you." She held out an impatient hand. "Come on, Mr. Gamble. Are you able to to walk? If not, I'll carry you."

"I'm all right," he said. However, he was forced to accept her hand in order to rise.

"This way," she ordered. "Lean on me."

He did so gratefully; his legs seemed made of rubber. She placed an arm about his waist and half-led, half-carried him back the way he had come. He was conscious of the softness of her body against his, a softness which her strength belied. Necessity aside, it was pleasant to hold and to be held. More than mere sensuality, it was a reaffirmation of life. He wanted to tell her so but could not find the words. He settled for an incongruous compliment instead. "You smell nice."

"You don't," she replied bluntly. "You must have landed in some garbage when you fell."

She had left her motor scooter concealed in a doorway at the mouth of Via Mugnaio. "Climb on," she invited, starting the engine. "I'll take you home."

He got up behind her although the scooter appeared scarcely large enough for one. She instructed him to clasp her waist. He would have done so, anyway. While she claimed not to be a Roman, she drove like one, at breakneck speed, often on the wrong side of the street and without slowing at intersections.

As they left Trastevere and hurtled across the Palatine bridge, she turned her helmeted head to speak to him. "A little lower, please."

Without realizing it, he had been gripping her breasts. He lowered his hands quickly. "Sorry," he muttered.

"I don't really mind," she told him with a grin. "But you were beginning to squeeze. Does my driving frighten you?"

"Of course not," he replied. And regretted the lie since she promptly increased their speed. "But Senso Unico . . . doesn't that mean it's a one-way street?"

She nodded—and kept right on going. "It's only for a little way."

He hoped she was right. After what seemed an eternity, the scooter began to slow. A moment later, the breakneck ride was over. "Here we are," she announced.

155

Gamble gazed around at their unexpected destination, a small irregularly shaped square embracing an even smaller park and bordered by apartment buildings. "Where's here?"

"Piazza Galeria. Home. My home, that is. Under the circumstances, I thought you'd be safer here than at the Pensione Danesi." She added with a smile for the deception he had attempted that afternoon, "Or at the Hilton, either."

He was too weary to object even if there had been any logical reason to do so. The assassin, foiled once, might strike again out of the darkness. Tomorrow he would be able to protect himself. Tonight, bruised and shaken, he could not. She offered him a security which had little to do with the pistol in her purse, the security of a friend, probably the only one he had in the city if not the entire world. He shambled after her as she wheeled the scooter into the lobby of the nearest building and down a wide corridor to a door at the rear.

Behind it lay a studio apartment, a living room containing a couch which converted into a double bed, a tiny kitchenette, a bath with a tub (and, inevitably, a bidet) but no shower. The furnishings were a combination of old and new, cheap and expensive. The ornately carved sideboard looked like an antique, but a plastic-encased television sat beside it. And although she apparently lived here alone, the decor was not overtly feminine save for the articles of clothing strewed carelessly about.

She removed the crash helmet and shook her taffy-colored hair. "You're a mess," she pronounced. "You could use a hot bath. And so could your clothes. Give them to me and I'll put them in the washer."

He tried a wan smile. "I didn't bring along a change."

"That wasn't very farsighted of you," she told him with mock reproof. "A good thing that one of us is prepared for emergencies." She produced a pair of folded pajamas from the sideboard. "These should fit you." They were a man's pajamas but she did not identify the owner and he thought it impolite to ask. "I'll have coffee ready when you're finished. Or something stronger if you prefer."

"Coffee will be fine." He hesitated.

"Well?" She regarded him impishly. "Would you like me to undress you?"

"I can probably handle that for myself."

"Then what's bothering you?"

"You've saved my life, you're offering me a bath and clean clothes, and I guess you mean for me to sleep here, too . . . so isn't it about time you told me your name?"

When he emerged from the bathroom, his soiled clothing was sloshing in the washing machine and a pot of coffee was steaming on the stove. The young woman had donned her own pajamas. She sat cross-legged on the open sofa bed, a newspaper in her lap. "Feel better?" she asked.

"Cleaner, anyway." Soap and hot water had removed the grime but not the pain. His throat still burned and his head still ached; in addition, his knees were bruised and there was a sore spot in the middle of his back where the assassin's knee had pressed. "Thank you, Rayah—for everything. By the way, what sort of a name is Rayah Zaporov? Russian?"

"My parents were Russian. I'm Israeli. I was born in Haifa." She patted the bed beside her, inviting him to join her. Except for the scooter, there was no other place to sit in the cramped living room.

"What are you doing in Rome?" Gamble asked. "I'm assuming that you're not really a student at the University."

"As a matter of fact, I am—among other things. "

"Such as what? Guardian angel for stray tourists?"

157

"Oh, come on," Rayah reproved. "You're not exactly a tourist, Gus. I know you're working on a MUF case for your atomic agency."

"What's MUF?" he replied with pretended bewilderment.

She laughed. "Material unaccounted for—as if you didn't know. You don't have to play games with me. We're on the same side. I belong to Mossad. You're afraid that the missing plutonium has been made into a bomb. So are we."

"I see," he murmured. The Israeli intelligence apparatus, although small in comparison to those of the superpowers, was highly respected. Yet its sphere of operations was usually limited to matters of immediate national concern. "No, that's wrong. I don't see at all. What is Israel's interest in this?"

"My country is in an extremely vulnerable position. Especially in the area of nuclear attack and subversion. Because of that we maintain certain contacts within the IAEA. When we learned that you were here—and why you were here— we thought we'd better involve ourselves. If there's a nuclear bomb floating about, we have to know it."

"Even though the bomb isn't intended for Israel?"

"The past thirty years have taught us not to take chances. We remember Munich—and that, right here in Rome, PLO terrorists planned to use a heat-seeking missile to shoot down an El Al airliner."

Gamble chuckled mirthlessly. "Maybe I should have come to you in the first place. I haven't been able to convince my own country or Italy that there's anything to worry about."

She assumed at first that he was exaggerating. Even after he had told her the whole story—he saw no reason not to— she continued to shake her taffy hair incredulously. "To fight the enemy is hard enough. But to have to fight your friends also . . ."

"Do you think I'm out of my mind, Rayah?"

158

"No, I think you may be the only sane one of the lot." She smiled. "Although a bit of a fool, perhaps. You should never have gone to Trastevere alone. If I hadn't been ordered to follow you—"

"I know. I'd be lying dead in Via Mugnaio."

"Your mistake was that you don't understand the local customs. Bribing the hospital clerk was quite acceptable behavior. But you paid him too much for the reason you gave. That started him thinking. If you were willing to pay twenty thousand lire for Simon Stone's address, perhaps Simon Stone would pay more to keep it a secret. So he contacted Stone, who suggested that he send you to Trastevere—where Stone was waiting for you."

"It wasn't Stone," Gamble muttered. "Just Stone's executioner." The picture of Maggi Lane's contorted purplish face rose in his memory. No fortuitous interruption had saved her from the rope. He shuddered.

Rayah touched his cheek comfortingly. "You'll be more careful from now on. And, actually, the fact that you were attacked tonight is a blessing in disguise. It proves that you're on the right track."

"Does it?" he replied gloomily. "To you and me, yes, But do you know what it will prove to Fuselli? Absolutely nothing. He'll say I simply wandered down a dark alley and got mugged by somebody after my wallet. I can't prove that Stone had anything to do with it. You can bet that he doesn't live at Seventy-nine Via Mugnaio and never did. And Caccavale—if he's still in town—will deny that he ever saw me, much less set me up. It's no use, Rayah. Unless"—he hesitated—"you'd be willing to back me up. Fuselli might listen to me then."

"I can't do that. I'd have to identify myself to Fuselli as a Mossad agent. That would jeopardize our whole apparatus here."

"You see?" he said with a hopeless shrug. "Everybody's got a reason for keeping their hands off. It's still just me against the world. And the world is winning."

"You're tired, Gus. You'll feel better in the morning."

"I'm more than just tired. I'm whipped."

"You're tired," she repeated and took his hands. "Tired and cold and lonely. Your mind is filled with death. It's chilled you to the bone. You need to warm yourself. You need to forget death for a little while, to taste life again." She sought to pull him to her and, feeling him resist, said, "Don't ask me to believe you don't want me. I know that you do. I knew it this afternoon."

He avoided her eyes. "I won't deny it. But that doesn't matter."

"My dear, it's the only thing that does matter."

"There's one fact about me that I didn't tell you, Rayah. I'm also a Catholic priest."

"So?" She cupped his chin with her hand and forced him to confront her smile, a smile both sensual and at the same time oddly maternal. "I'm sure God will understand that tonight you're only a man. Trust me, Gus. After all, we've known Him a lot longer than you have."

And in the morning he did feel better, just as Rayah had promised. Much better, he thought, than he had any right to feel. He had violated his vow of chastity and would, no doubt, be punished for it. But at this moment the sense of guilt was strangely lacking; he was filled instead with a strange sort of peace. He felt cleansed rather than defiled. Last night he had been a beaten animal. The strangler's rope had not taken his life but it had come close to breaking his spirit. This morning he was a man again, able to take up the battle. For this he could thank the woman. Whether moved by passion or compassion, she had healed him. Twice she had reached out to save him from the darkness . . . and who could say with confidence which had been the more important?

"I'm glad," she said when he told her. She had arisen while he was still sleeping and had gone shopping for their breakfast—sweet-tasting melon and rolls still warm from the oven. They sat at a tiny table in the kitchenette, their knees touching. But the darkness had gone and the sun had risen and their intimacy was that of friends, not lovers. "But I really didn't plan it that way, Gus. I'm not that wise. I simply felt that it was right. For you—and for me, too."

"Then it was more than just sympathy?"

"Much more. With you, I could feel . . . well, a little less lonely, perhaps."

"A pretty girl like you—lonely? You must know lots of other men, younger and—"

"What on earth does age have to do with it?" she interrupted with a trace of impatience. "Of course, I know other men. I could sleep with someone every night if I chose. I'm not boasting. Nearly any female can say the same. But it doesn't ease the loneliness. It's only when I can be important to someone the way I was to you last night, the way I used to be . . ."

Her parents, Rayah told him, had been killed in a terrorist raid on a settlement in northern Galilee, along with an older brother. Her husband had died in the Yom Kippur war. At an age when most American girls were still in school, she was already a widow and an orphan. However, she was by no means unique; in her small embattled nation, there were many like her. "For a while, I felt very sorry for myself," she admitted dispassionately. "I thought my life was over. Can you imagine feeling that way at nineteen? I finally saw how ridiculous that was. My life hadn't ended, it had simply changed. I had to do something with it so I volunteered for military service. Because I'm fluent in several languages, they

161

put me into Mossad." She had served as an agent for nearly five years, the last two in Rome.

"Do you enjoy the work?"

She shrugged. "Occasionally, it makes me feel useful. But I don't deceive myself. Anyone could do what I do, perhaps better than I."

"Then why not let them? Haven't you ever thought of remarrying?"

"Is that a proposal?" she asked with a mischievous grin. "Don't turn pale, Gus. I'm only joking. I don't want to make any more lasting commitments. Not to you, not to anyone."

Her vehemence did not entirely convince him. Rayah wore self-sufficiency like a shell but he had seen beneath that shell and he suspected that at the right time the right man might cause her to abandon it. But he was not that man. So all he said was, "I just want you to know that I'll never forget you."

"That sounds like you're saying good-bye."

"There's work to be done. Thanks to you, I'm still alive to do it."

"But how? Last night you were so positive that no one would listen to you."

"That was last night. This morning it occurs to me that maybe I've been talking to the wrong people." He smiled crookedly. "It's a funny question for a Catholic to ask a Jew —but how does one go about getting a papal audience?"

The answer, he rapidly discovered, was that one did not. Even on an ordinary day, the Bishop of Rome granted private audiences only to the most prominent and influential. And this was no ordinary day. It was Good Friday when the shepherd of the world's 600 million Roman Catholics would lead his flock—in person and via global television—in solemn observance of the crucifixion nineteen centuries earlier. The notion that he might interrupt his duties, which included

162

a liturgical service in St. Peter's Cathedral and a procession around the Colosseum, to meet an insignificant visitor from the United States struck everyone who heard it as preposterous. Gamble was shuffled from one minor Vatican functionary to another, always with the same result.

However, in the church as elsewhere, it is often not a question of what you know but whom you know. His dogged (and unauthorized) use of Francis Inman's name finally reached a friendly ear. Emilio Mattei had worked with Inman during Vatican II and considered the American his good friend. Mattei now served as an upper level official with the Curia Romana, the powerful bureaucracy which assisted the Pope in the government and operation of the church.

Mattei, a brisk priest-administrator, assumed that his visitor was there as Inman's representative. As such, Gamble was made welcome to his office whose windows overlooked the verdant gardens of the Vatican. "I'm disappointed that my dear brother Francis did not advise me of your coming. It would have given me much pleasure to see that you were properly accommodated."

"To be honest with you, Father Frank doesn't know I'm here."

Mattei listened to his explanation with unfeigned astonishment. Now and then he smiled nervously, as though suspecting that a joke was being played upon him. When Gamble had finished, he said cautiously, "Let me be certain I understand. You are a priest and, at the same time, a police officer?"

"That's correct."

"And yet, by your own admission, you have no authority save your own to act in either capacity. As a priest, you were ordered to return to your parish, an order which you have disobeyed. As a police officer, you were relieved of duty, an action which you have ignored."

"I've explained my reasons, Father Emilio."

"Um," Mattei replied dubiously. His life was built on the cornerstone of obedience to authority; he did not condone rebellion easily. "Well, be that as it may, you are asking me to arrange an audience with His Holiness—in order that you might warn him of a threat to his life."

"His life—and the lives of a lot of other people."

"So you would have me believe." Mattei eyed him skeptically. "By an odd coincidence, I happen to know Simon Stone. During the time he worked in Rome, I met him on several occasions. Frankly, I was greatly impressed by him. Do you know what impressed me the most? His immense love for the church."

"I believe he still loves it—in his own warped fashion."

"That doesn't make sense. One does not destroy what one loves."

"I don't think Stone really intends to destroy the church, only those he believes have led it astray. Maybe that doesn't make sense to you or me, Father Emilio. But Stone is mentally ill."

"Are you also a psychiatrist, then?"

"No," Gamble admitted. "But I do know something about human behavior. There's no other way to account for Stone's actions."

"Forgive me for saying so," Mattei murmured, "but there are some who might consider your own behavior in this matter to be—shall we say?—peculiar."

"Is it peculiar to want to prevent a terrible tragedy? If so, I'm guilty."

"I don't doubt your sincerity. However, able and experienced men, men of equal sincerity, have investigated your accusations against Simon Stone and found them baseless." Mattei shook his head slowly. "I have heard nothing to persuade me that they are mistaken."

"What do you want? Stone's written confession? 'How I plan to blow up the—'" He stopped, his eyes narrowing. "Maybe that's not as ridiculous as it sounds."

"I'm afraid I don't follow you."

"I'm putting myself in Stone's place . . . He doesn't see himself as your ordinary, garden variety terrorist, the sort who strikes without warning. No, he sees himself as a prophet, a modern Jeremiah. One thing about prophets, they always make a lot of noise. They thunder and denounce, they give the sinner one last chance to recant." He sat forward in his chair. "Father Emilio, has His Holiness received any threatening communications in the past few days?"

"I'm not aware of any."

"Could you find out?"

Mattei hesitated. "I suppose there's no harm in it," he said finally. "And if it will serve to end the matter . . ." He made a telephone call to another office and, shortly, a bulky file envelope was delivered by a runner. While Gamble leafed through it, he explained, "Because of his position, the Holy Father receives a certain number of crank letters, including threats. We pay no attention to them, of course."

"I think you'd better pay attention to this one," Gamble said, passing a single sheet of typewritten paper to Mattei. According to the stamp, the message had arrived only the day before.

Mattei put on his spectacles and read the letter aloud. " 'To the Bishop of Rome: Hear the judgment of Almighty God! You have been weighed and found wanting. Under your corrupt stewardship, the universal church which the Lord entrusted to you has broken his commandments and gone whoring after false gods. You have fashioned a golden calf which you bid his people worship and which is a stench and an abomination in his sight. False priests grow fat and prosperous while everywhere his children sicken and die.

The warnings of his prophet go unheeded. But know that the hour of their deliverance is at hand. The cruel yoke shall be lifted and righteousness restored. Harken, therefore, and obey! You will stand before the multitudes on the sacred day of resurrection and proclaim a rebirth of the Holy Church. You will cease to lay up treasure for yourself here on earth but, humbly confessing your most grievous sin, divest yourself of your ill-gotten wealth and, true to the commandment of our Savior, Jesus the Christ, sell all that you have and give to the poor. Yet should you persist in your arrogance, be warned that God is a jealous god and not to be mocked. His vengeance shall descend upon you from on high and the manner of it shall be terrible indeed.' "

"Well, that's plain enough," Gamble observed softly. "Stone has picked Easter as the target date. That gives us something less than forty-eight hours."

Mattei smiled indulgently. "Surely, you don't take this garbage seriously. Give me the file. I can show you much worse than that—and nothing ever came of them."

"They didn't have a ploot bomb. Stone does."

"There is no signature," Mattei pointed out. "How can you be sure that Simon Stone wrote it?"

"The tone is right and so is the timing. Those are Stone's sentiments, from A to Z. Now will you arrange for me to speak with the Pope?"

Mattei shook his head. "That's utterly impossible."

"Then will you speak to him?"

"I fear you overrate my importance. At this particular time, the Holy Father sees only his closest advisers. Most of his waking hours, in fact, are spent in prayer and fasting. Following Easter, of course, the situation will improve and then perhaps—"

"Following Easter!" Gamble echoed despairingly. "My God, don't you understand that 'following Easter' will be too

166

late? We're not debating how many angels can dance on the head of a pin. We're talking about survival!"

"Calm yourself," Mattei replied sharply. "I have listened patiently. Your insolence wearies me. I must ask you to leave."

"I'm not being insolent, Father Emilio. And I'm not leaving until I've convinced someone to take me seriously."

The ultimatum made Mattei flush. He regarded Gamble in grim silence. Then, surprisingly, he smiled. "Since you insist," he said softly. "I believe I know who that someone should be." He left the office. When he returned, nearly ten minutes later, two other men were with him. "This is the person," he told them, indicating Gamble with a wave of his hand. "Please escort him to the gate."

"You don't mean you're having me arrested!"

"Only if you refuse to go quietly."

"But what about the letter? Aren't you going to do anything about it?"

"I will inform my superiors, of course." Mattei sighed. "But I will not be surprised if they reach the same conclusion as I. That, in view of your irrational behavior, you may well have written it yourself."

Rayah was waiting for him in the shade of the Bernini colonnades which embraced the piazza of St. Peter's like two marble arms.

The vast square, as usual, teemed with motion, tour buses arriving and departing, little cars circling the perimeter in search of parking, and bicycle and motor scooters swooping about the twin fountains and the Fontana obelisk as gracefully as the pigeons overhead . . . bringing the foreigner and the native, the reverent and the merely curious to Christendom's largest church. Ironically, its size had not actually been conceived to the glory of God but to the vanity of man.

167

Julius II had wished a structure large enough to house his sumptuous tomb which, a further irony, was never built.

Few of the visitors were aware of this. Nor would they have cared. It was enough for them that the mighty basilica existed, whatever its origins; for one-sixth the world's population, this was the church of churches. Confronting its majesty, they moved at first uncertainly, pausing to contemplate the imposing façade and to lift their eyes to the huge dome, the highest on earth, looming 452 feet above the street—then, as though the square had a prevailing current, to drift toward the towering doors. Although the flow was constant, the number in the piazza never seemed to diminish. Each departing pilgrim was immediately replaced by another.

"Yes, it's always like this," Rayah assured him. "But what you see now is nothing compared with what it will be on Easter morning. They begin to gather before dawn. By noon —when the Pope delivers his message from that balcony— the piazza will be jammed from one side to the other. Perhaps a hundred thousand people, packed in like sardines."

"Then I guess I'd better pray for rain."

"It won't make a bit of difference." Her eyes narrowed. "Is that when it's going to happen, Gus? Here—on Easter morning?"

"That depends on who you prefer to believe—me or the rest of the world."

"Oh, dear," she murmured. "You mean they wouldn't listen to you, either?"

"I've finally learned who it is I'm fighting, Rayah. It isn't Stone, he's almost secondary. It's good men with no imagination. It's bureaucrats who might lose their jobs if they create a fuss. It's all those people who want quick and easy solutions to any problem—and the quickest and easiest is to pretend that the problem doesn't exist. You see, nothing like this has ever happened before. For most people, that's proof that it

168

never will. To their way of thinking, nothing ever happens for the first time. If there's no historical precedent, forget it."

"Did you ever stop to consider," Rayah said thoughtfully, "that disasters may be God's way of getting our attention? It's the only method that seems to work."

"Maybe. But I don't think we should accept a disaster as God's will until we've done everything humanly possible to prevent it."

"Haven't you? Isn't it time you faced the truth—that people who won't be saved, can't be saved?" She took his hands, her expression earnest. "At least save yourself, Gus. Let's run away. We can be in Venice in a few hours. It's a marvelous city for lovers, a place where you can forget the world and its troubles. Or we can go even farther if you'd like—to Switzerland, or Austria."

"I thought you didn't want to make any long-term commitments, Rayah."

"I didn't say positively." Then, slowly, she released his hands. "You're not going to leave, are you? You intend to stay here and be slaughtered with the rest of the sheep."

"I can't leave until it's over. One way or another."

"Maybe they're right," she said despairingly. "Maybe you are crazy."

"Of course, they're right." He forced a smile. "Wait till you get a load of me on Easter morning. If all else fails, I'm going to dress up in a long robe and march around the piazza with a big sign. 'The World Will End at Noon or Thereabouts. Those Not Interested in Participating, Follow Me to . . .' Where's a good place to hide, Rayah?"

She smiled also, humoring him. "For a hundred thousand people? My apartment's out of the question. Would you consider the Colosseum?"

"Too small—and rundown, besides. How about the subway? Never mind, we'll use the catacombs. They saved a lot of Christians in their day. What's the biggest and the best? I wouldn't want to lead my people to a dump."

"San Callisto, I suppose." She grimaced, tired of the game. "Don't talk nonsense, Gus."

"Why not? I've tried talking sense and that's no fun." She didn't understand that his pent-up frustration must be vented in some fashion or that his laughter was perilously close to tears. "Hey, how about this for a catchy slogan? 'Don't Stay Here and Get Stoned! Amble with Gamble to San Callisto!' Set it to music and—" He stopped suddenly. His eyes, though still fixed on the woman's face, no longer saw it. "San Callisto," he repeated with no trace of his previous flippancy.

She regarded him curiously. "What is it?"

"I'm not sure. Tell me about San Callisto."

"Well, it's one of the biggest of the catacombs. Only a part of it is open to the public. There must be several miles of tunnels on different levels." She paused, puzzled by the intensity of his gaze, half-suspecting that he was still clowning. "Even so, I doubt if a hundred thousand people could hide in it."

"How about five?" He didn't wait for a reply but grabbed her by the waist and began to dance jubilantly about the thick marble columns. "How about one, two, three, four, five!"

"Gus!" she gasped. "What on earth are you doing?"

"Celebrating." He released his grasp but kept his foolish grin. "I've been so busy worrying about what Stone was going to do that I completely forgot what he's already done. He spent a year in Rome, studying the history of the early church. He even wrote a treatise about it—and a damned good one, according to Father Frank. Want to guess what the subject was? The Catacombs of San Callisto, that's what!"

170

"So?"

"So put yourself in Stone's shoes. You come to Rome with a bomb in your pocket. You and your friends need a place to stay until you're ready to use it. You're not too particular where because, as far as you know, nobody's on your trail. Maybe you rent a quiet little pensione where you can come and go without attracting attention. After all, the town's knee-deep in foreigners. Then you hear there's another American looking for you. You begin to worry. Could the guy be a cop? Maybe, maybe not—in any case, you'd better play it safe by getting rid of him, just like you got rid of Maggi Lane. But your luck is bad this time and the guy gets away. Now you're really worried. Now you need more than a place to stay. You need a hole to hide in. If you're Simon Stone, what hole comes to mind?"

"Not San Callisto. It's too public, people going in and out all the time—"

"Didn't you just tell me that there are miles of tunnels and that most of them are off limits to the public? I'll bet they weren't off limits to a church scholar. I'll bet Stone knows San Callisto like the back of his hand, which tunnels are being used and which aren't, how to get in and out without being seen. It feels right, Rayah." He took her arm. "Let's go."

She held back. "You're not thinking of going in there alone, are you?"

"I may be crazy but I'm not stupid." He touched his throat gingerly; it was still painful. "When I stick my neck out this time, I mean to have plenty of company."

The
Lair

QUESTURA CENTRALE, Rome's central police headquarters, was situated amid a clutch of other government buildings on Via San Vitale, not far from the railway station. Lacking official clout (and unwilling to disclose his business to underlings), Gamble anticipated difficulty in gaining an interview with Ugo Fuselli. To his surprise, his name was entree enough. He was passed rapidly upward along the chain of command until he reached the office of the deputy chief.

"Thank you for coming," Fuselli greeted him suavely. "How kind of you to spare me the necessity of having to search for you."

"I didn't dream you cared, Colonel."

"Ah, but I do. An hour ago I received a telephone call from a Father Mattei at the Vatican. From him I learned that you are determined to make a nuisance of yourself. I warned you what the consequences would be." Fuselli held out his hand. "Your passport, please."

172

"You can't deport me. Not now."

"Can't I?" Fuselli depressed the intercom key. "Rocco, as soon as the deportation order is completed, bring it to me for signature. And prepare an escort to Fiumicino." He gave Gamble a bleak smile. "All that remains is to wish you a pleasant journey—which, in my opinion, is more than you deserve."

"Oh, I know you have the power," Gamble acknowledged. "But I don't believe you're stupid enough to use it after you hear what I'm going to tell you."

"More of your hallucinations? Spare me, please."

"Does this look like an hallucination?" He bared his throat to reveal the livid marks left by the noose. "I'd like to file a complaint of attempted murder."

"Against whom?"

"Last night I got Simon Stone's address and went looking for him. One of his gang ambushed me. It had to be Yvarra, the man who strangled Maggi Lane." He quickly sketched in the rest of the story, omitting only the part Rayah had played in it and attributing his escape instead to the chance intervention of a passerby.

Fuselli was unimpressed. "Your obsession with the man Stone has clouded your reason. The truth is that what happened to you could have happened to anyone. Especially a tourist—and especially in Trastevere." He added, "That is, of course, if it actually happened at all."

"Is this how you treat all victims who come to you, Colonel?"

"Only those I know to be confirmed liars." Fuselli picked up a pencil. "However, your complaint will be investigated in the normal manner. Let us begin with witnesses. What was the name of the passerby who saved you?"

"I don't know," Gamble said, thereby somewhat substantiating Fuselli's derogatory characterization. "In the confusion, I didn't get it."

"And the name of the clerk at the hospital whom you claim to have bribed—no doubt you were too confused to learn that, also."

"No. But please, Colonel, let's not waste time. The attack on me isn't really important except that it points the way ..." He saw Fuselli's bored expression and he sighed. "Okay, have it your way. The clerk's name is Caccavale, Bruno Caccavale."

"Bruno Caccavale," Fuselli repeated; it seemed to Gamble that there was a new note in his voice. "Are you certain?"

"Would I make up a name like Bruno Caccavale? Young fellow, maybe twenty-five, with dark hair and a scar on his left cheek. But I doubt if you'll get anything out of him. Bruno's a worse liar than I am. Richer, too."

There was a discreet knock on the door and the secretary Rocco entered. He carried an official-looking paper. "I have the deportation order, Colonel. And the escort you ordered is waiting."

Fuselli's hand accepted the document but his eyes remained fixed on Gamble's face. "Thank you," he said absently. "Rocco, what was the name of the man we fished out of the Tiber this morning—near the Ponte Sublica?"

"The Sicilian hospital attendant? Bruno Caccavale." It was Rocco's responsibility to have such information at his fingertips. "The report is on my desk. Shall I get it?"

Fuselli shook his head. "You may go, Rocco."

A short silence followed his departure. Gamble was the one who broke it. "Shall I guess how Caccavale died?"

"He was garroted," Fuselli said slowly, "and his body thrown into the river."

"Aren't you going to accuse me of doing it?"

Fuselli sighed. "It appears that I may owe you an apology."

174

"Would you mind putting it in writing? It'll give me something to read on the plane."

Fuselli became aware that he was still holding the deportation order. He dropped it carefully into the wastebasket. "I think you'll be staying with us a bit longer, after all. In fact, I insist on it."

"I thought you'd never ask." He smiled wryly. "Funny. Last night I'd have cheerfully strangled Bruno myself. Today I'd like to thank him. If he hadn't made the mistake of trying to play both ends against the middle . . ."

"His mistake," Fuselli agreed. "And Simon Stone's. It would have been wiser simply to have paid him off. Without his death to corroborate your story—"

"Stone's policy is to leave no witnesses. Towler, Yontis, Maggi Lane . . . If he knocks off just me, Bruno may talk. But if he kills both of us, he's in the clear. Two unrelated homicides—you'd never have made the connection. Unfortunately for him, I got away." He chuckled. "Goes to prove that killing two birds with one Stone isn't as easy as it's cracked up to be."

The idiom lost something in the translation. Fuselli didn't smile. "You are a very lucky man. All of us are, in fact."

"That remains to be seen. It's only Good Friday. Easter is still coming."

"The Vatican must be warned that a threat exists," Fuselli muttered. "Embarrassing, to say the least . . . since I just finished assuring them in the strongest possible terms that your story was utter rubbish."

"Warning the Vatican is fine for openers. What next?"

"It appears to me that we have one advantage. We know the target and the hour it is to be attacked. This permits us to concentrate our forces, construct a defense. I will put a cordon around Vatican City which not even a mouse will be able to penetrate."

"That isn't enough, Colonel. Conventional procedures didn't stop Stone from stealing the ploot. They won't stop him from delivering it."

Fuselli licked his lips uneasily. "What do you propose?"

"That we go on the offensive. Don't wait for him to come to us. Go after him, instead." Gamble got to his feet. "How long since you've visited the catacombs, Colonel?"

It had always been a cemetery although not originally, as many supposed, a Christian one. The practice of interring the dead in subterranean chambers had originated with the Etruscans, many centuries before Christ. The Romans adopted the practice and improved upon it. Where the Etruscans were content to build individual tombs which resembled a small house, the Romans hewed out whole underground cities, vast labyrinths of galleries and intersecting tunnels, often on several different levels. The rich and the powerful were laid to rest in apartment-sized vaults. Those less fortunate in life fared no better in death. They were buried in the gallery walls, one above the next, as many as twelve deep. Only much later did the catacombs (a Roman word meaning "the hollows," a reference to the shallow valley in which the first was located) become a refuge for the living as well as the dead. The Christian minority found the intricate mazes admirably suited for concealment from their persecutors and, in secretly constructed chapels, they practiced the forbidden sacraments. By the fourth century, however, the catacombs had been abandoned for both burial and sanctuary and for the next millennium were nearly forgotten. Then, rediscovered and restored, they became a mecca for the pilgrim and the archaeologist—and, more recently, the tourist.

The Catacombs of San Callisto, named for an early pope, was situated in the Ardeantine section south of the city and close to Via Appia Antica, the fabled Appian Way which had already been old when it echoed to the tread of Caesar's legions and the rumble of his chariots. At first glance, the site was not impressive. It held none of the dilapidated grandeur of the Colosseum; the melancholy sense of history which hangs over the Forum or the Caracallan Baths was absent. The stranger might conclude that what he saw was only a barren field—too large for the two buildings it embraced—and wonder why such valuable real estate would be allowed to remain unused, without ever suspecting what lay beneath his feet.

By night, there was even less to see. But tonight's visitors were not sightseers, anyway. San Callisto was ringed with a small army of carabinieri and the roads surrounding it closed to traffic. The last tourist had departed earlier; the resident caretakers had been removed without explanation. Heavily armed guards were posted at each of the catacomb's emergency exits, although only one—a former sand quarry nearly a mile south of the main entrance—showed any evidence that it had been used in the past decade.

The strike force which gathered at the bunkerlike entrance consisted of two dozen of Fuselli's most seasoned officers plus, at Gamble's suggestion, a bomb disposal squad. The men wore dark-colored jumpsuits, flak jackets and steel helmets. In addition to his weapons, carbine and pistol, each man carried a miner's torch and a gas mask.

Fuselli divided his men into teams of three and passed out maps marked to show the areas each team would explore. "Be thorough but be cautious," he warned. "When you've completed searching your sector, remain there and wait for further orders. I don't want any would-be hero wandering about and perhaps getting shot by his comrades."

He drew Gamble aside. "There is no reason you should go with us. Especially since you refuse to carry a gun. You've done enough, my friend. Wait here where you'll be safe."

177

"Can you guarantee I'll be any safer up here than down there?"

Fuselli eyed him soberly. "Perhaps not." Uppermost in the minds of both men was the possibility that Simon Stone might choose to detonate his bomb in a final apocalyptic gesture rather than surrender it. In that case, little would remain of San Callisto and anyone in its vicinity, whether above the ground or below it. "Come along, then. And let us pray that God protects us all."

"I didn't think a Communist was supposed to believe in God."

"I don't," Fuselli replied briefly. "But why take chances?"

Single file, they entered the mouth of the catacomb. The staircase was constructed of wood and the walls of the shaft which enclosed it were stuccoed, giving the impression that they were descending into the basement of an old house. The steps terminated in a small room with a hard-packed earthen floor. From it tunnels branched off in several directions, the uppermost of San Callisto's seven levels and the only one most visitors ever saw.

"It's not likely we'll find anyone here," Fuselli said. "However, don't let that make you careless." He gave Gamble the ghost of a smile. "Incredible as it may seem, I am sometimes mistaken."

In this case, he was not. A sweep of the first level turned up nothing. The strike force descended to the second level. Although they now stood at a depth where the sun's rays never penetrated, the air was still fresh and the temperature remained at an acceptable 62 degrees. It was not the cold but anticipation that made Gamble shiver.

Here again only the dead awaited them. The galleries, little more than a yard wide, appeared to have been laid out in haphazard fashion, intersecting with one another at irregular angles. They were bored in solid stone which needed no braces, the *tufa litoide* from which Rome's ancient buildings (and, indeed, many of its modern ones as well) were constructed. They were lined on both sides with individual graves, called loculi, some containing as many as four bodies and closed by slabs of marble or by huge tiles cemented together. A few bore engraved epitaphs but most of the grave markers had been merely painted and were long since obliterated, their occupants forever anonymous. Spaced regularly along the tunnels were the cubicula, family vaults like tiny apartments, some still containing remnants of murals which spoke of the occupants' earthly accomplishments.

As they slowly worked their way deeper, the character of the catacomb changed perceptibly. On its upper level, San Callisto was primarily a cemetery. Below, it was still that but something more besides, a place of refuge and of worship. Here they found larger rooms which were not cubicula but chapels with stone altars and religious symbols carved into the walls.

The search was now over two hours old; it had covered five of the seven levels and it had still not turned up a trace of the quarry. "What do you think?" Fuselli asked anxiously. "Have we struck a dry well?"

"We haven't reached bottom yet. They're here."

"If so, let's hope that they haven't become aware that we're here, too." Descending from one level to the next was especially perilous. The police, crowded together on the narrow steps and made clearly visible by their electric torches, would be easy targets for an enemy waiting in the darkness. An ambush would not alter the final outcome—the hijackers, outnumbered and in a trap, had no chance of escape—but it would increase the number of casualties, perhaps (if worse came to worst) astronomically.

Surprise was still on their side. Moving with all the stealth two dozen men could muster, they reached the sixth level.

And there, as they clustered in the low-ceilinged anteroom preparatory to fanning out in teams, Gamble's nostrils detected a new odor in the musty air. A moment later, he identified it and caught Fuselli's arm but the Italian had already made the same discovery.

"Candle smoke!" he whispered. "We've found them!"

Not quite. The modern fugitives, like their ancient Christian counterparts, had been forced to rely on candles to illuminate their burrow. But the acrid smell, drifting slowly through the tunnels, had no immediately identifiable source. Their quarry might be anywhere in the maze, around the next corner or a quarter mile distant.

Fuselli put a finger to his lips, enjoining his men to silence, and pointed to the tunnel each team was to investigate. There was a final check of weapons, most of the men crossed themselves (Fuselli among them, Gamble noted) and the strike teams began to move out.

Fuselli had reserved for his own team the most likely area, the level's main gallery. It ran straight for perhaps fifty yards, then was intersected by another gallery equally wide; together, they formed a cross. Around the hub were clustered larger chambers which had served in bygone days as chapels, congregational meeting places and even baptistries. Logic suggested that five men, given their choice of living quarters, could reasonably be expected to select the most spacious. And in corroboration, the smell of burning candles seemed to grow stronger with each step.

A more impetuous leader might have regarded this as the signal to charge. Fuselli, the coolly methodical professional, resisted the temptation. He continued to lead his team forward in the same deliberate fashion he had displayed throughout the long search, leaving nothing to chance. Fearing they might yet blunder into a trap, he approached each cubicula as if it contained the enemy, reassuring himself that

180

it was empty before beckoning the others to proceed.

The conservative course was the correct one under the circumstances . . . but, in the end, paid no more dividends than recklessness. As they neared the spot where the two galleries intersected, one of the officers stumbled on the uneven floor. Seeking to right himself, he dislodged his steel helmet. It fell with a clang which reverberated in the silence like a clap of thunder.

The figure of a man appeared in an arched doorway, too far beyond the beam of their lamps to be more than an indistinct shadow. Apparently, he couldn't see any better than he could be seen because he called in English, "Hey, Simon! That you?"

Fuselli's fist punched Gamble's shoulder. "Yeah," he called back in the same language. "It's me."

The deception failed. "Like hell!" the man exclaimed, his voice rising in sudden alarm. "It's the goddam cops!"

"Throw up your hands!" Fuselli yelled. "You are surrounded!"

Since in his excitement he spoke in Italian, perhaps he was understood, perhaps not. In any case, the answer was a shot.

"Lights out!" Fuselli bellowed, realizing that their lamps made them ready targets. "Get down!"

The order came an instant too late. Before it could be obeyed, there was a second shot. The officer who had dropped his helmet grunted loudly and lurched sideways. Gamble caught him and they fell to the floor together. In the pitch-darkness, it was impossible to determine either the location or the severity of the man's wound nor could he have done anything about it, anyway.

Both sides were firing now. The darkness was split by the flash of the guns and the tunnel reverberated to the overlapping explosions. Bullets spanged against the walls and floor and ceiling, ricocheting from the stone with the snarl of small deadly animals. To add to the din, Fuselli activated a hand-held siren to alert the rest of his force; its unearthly voice rose and fell like a keening banshee. There were human voices too, shouting orders and encouragement or raised suddenly in pain. Together, they created a deafening cacophony which was almost too painful for unprotected ears to endure. Gamble huddled on the cold floor while the man-made storm raged about him. On this cramped battlefield, it seemed improbable that anyone could escape the indiscriminate bullets.

And yet, miraculously, some did. The blind duel continued with unabated fury. Then all at once it slackened and Gamble realized that only the police carbines were still speaking.

"Hold your fire!" Fuselli roared. Still lying prone, he switched on his lamp, being careful to hold it well away from his body. The light drew no volley from the enemy. One of them, a tall man with sandy hair, sprawled face down in the tunnel; a bullet in the throat had nearly decapitated him. The legs of a second man, doubled in an unnatural position, were visible in the arched doorway to the chapel.

Fuselli turned off the siren. As its wail died away, they heard a new sound, rapidly receding, the sound of someone running away. Then there was a fresh burst of gunfire, its thunder muffled by distance and the intervening earth. One of the hijackers, seeking to escape the trap, had blundered into another of the strike teams.

"Three," Fuselli interpreted, his voice strangely loud in the sudden silence. "That leaves two."

"And the bomb," Gamble reminded him. He realized why Fuselli seemed to be shouting. It was in order to hear himself; the battle had left them all temporarily deafened. He raised his own voice. "The men don't matter. We've got to find the bomb."

Fuselli surveyed his team. "It appears that job belongs to

182

us, my friend." One of the officers, the man Gamble had caught while falling, was dead, shot squarely in the forehead. The other was wounded in the thigh. Although he had continued to fight despite it, he was plainly unable to walk.

They had to step over the two bodies to enter the chapel. Gamble identified the first from his sandy hair as Al Ziegler, the one-time Green Beret; his wound made his features unrecognizable. The second man, sprawled in the doorway, was the ex-machinist, Burt Troob.

A third man awaited them in the chapel. Unlike his companions, Tomás Yvarra was still alive. The Puerto Rican strangler sat on the floor, his back against the stone altar, his head drooping and his legs stuck out stiffly. His denim shirt was matted with blood. But it was not fresh blood. His wound was nearly twenty-four hours old and Rayah's pistol rather than police carbines had inflicted it. The crimson froth on his lips indicated that the bullet had pierced his lung; Gamble marveled that Yvarra had been able to flee. Only his magnificent physique had permitted it but, in the end, the result was the same. Unable to seek medical assistance, which might have saved him, Tomás Yvarra was dying.

However, a flicker of resistance remained. When the light struck him, he raised his massive head, squinting defiantly at his foes. A .45 caliber pistol was clenched in one hand. He attempted to lift it from his lap.

Fuselli wrenched the weapon from his grasp and tossed it into a corner. Kneeling, he cupped Yvarra's chin in his palm. "The bomb!" he snapped. "Where is it?"

A bloody bubble formed on Yvarra's lips, then burst at his whispered words. "Go to hell."

"After you," Fuselli retorted. "Answer me, damn you!"

"Never mind," Gamble said. "I think we've found it."

On top of the altar, almost seeming to be part of it, sat a gray metal box, the size of a small footlocker or perhaps a large tool kit. The hinged lid was fastened with two hasps and welded to it was an upright handle so that one man could carry it conveniently. The innocuous-looking box bore no warning legend but Gamble, regarding it raptly, felt sure that he had never before beheld anything quite so deadly.

Fuselli, staring also, murmured, "I expected it would be larger."

"It's large enough. Don't touch it. Wait for the bomb disposal people."

The remainder of the strike force was crowding into the chapel. With them, they carried yet another body, the hijacker who had attempted to flee. Gamble was not surprised to see that it was George Parker, the chemical engineer. The words which had greeted them—"Hey, Simon! That you?"—had already led him to suspect that Stone, the leader, was not with his comrades when the trap was sprung.

He squatted beside Yvarra and put his face close to that of the wounded man. "Tomás," he said gently, "you've been hurt bad—but we want to help you. Tell us where Stone is and we'll get you to a hospital."

"Screw you," Yvarra mumbled. Even though he was dying, the almost hypnotic spell which bound his disciples to the ex-priest still remained. "Gonna be all right. Gonna make the big score. Simon promised . . ."

"There's not going to be any big score, Tomás. There never was. Simon lied to you. He promised you lots of money —but it was all a lie. He used you. You don't owe him anything."

Yvarra didn't appear to understand. Then he sighed. "Son of a bitch." Gamble wasn't sure whether the curse was directed at his interrogator, at the leader who had deceived him or merely at himself, the lifetime loser. On the chance that it might also contain a plea for forgiveness, Gamble began swiftly, "I absolve you from your sins, in the name of the

Father and of the Son and of the Holy Spirit . . ."

The absolution went unacknowledged. Yvarra commenced to cough violently; then he was silent, eyes fixed blankly, the strangler choked on his own blood. Gamble got to his feet. "He's gone."

"Good riddance" was Fuselli's blunt opinion. "He has saved us the expense of both the doctor and the hangman." He motioned the bomb disposal squad forward. "Be careful how you handle it," he warned, indicating the metal box. "This is no time for an accident."

The remainder was unnecessary. While the others watched from a respectful distance, the squad spent nearly half an hour scrutinizing the box from all angles, listening to its innards with stethoscopes and testing its surface with various instruments before attempting to move it. Finally satisfied that the device was not booby-trapped, they lifted it gingerly from its resting place and placed it in a larger container brought along for the purpose. Then, walking with the utmost deliberation, they began to carry the awesome burden out of the catacomb.

With it, they took much of the tension. The gallery suddenly erupted with sound, men laughing and shouting and pounding each other on the back. "We've won!" Fuselli chortled, hugging Gamble in his exuberance. "It's over and we've won!"

"We haven't found Stone yet."

"You're a hard man to satisfy," Fuselli complained happily. "We've captured his bomb and we've eliminated his gang. Stone is beaten. He's nothing but a nuisance now. I tell you it's over, my friend."

"I guess it is." Yet he still could not quite accept the fact. He had lived with the nightmare too long; it had almost become a part of him. "Good work, Colonel."

"The credit belongs to you. You're a hero, man! You've

fought the whole world and you've won. Can't you even manage to smile about it?"

"I'm a little out of practice." Gamble sighed. "But give me time. I'll get the hang of it."

Rayah woke him at noon. From the catacomb, he had gone directly to the Piazza Galeria, not because he still feared an enemy but because he wished to share the good news with the one who, by saving his life, had made it possible. But accumulated fatigue, held at bay by excitement, would be denied no longer. He went to sleep sitting up, in the middle of his story. Rayah had put him to bed but he retained no recollection of it.

She greeted him with a smile. "How are you feeling by now, Gus? More like the conquering hero?"

"Maybe. I'm not sure I know how conquering heroes are supposed to feel."

"You'll learn," she predicted cheerfully. "Get dressed while I fix you something to eat. After that, we'll make some plans for the afternoon. A picnic at the beach, perhaps. It's a gorgeous day—and God knows you've earned the right to enjoy it."

He agreed. But when she looked in on him five minutes later, he was still sitting on the edge of the sofa bed, frowning at the floor. "What's wrong?" she inquired. "Are you ill?"

"I'm fine." He saw that she was unconvinced and he smiled sheepishly. "Okay, I'm not fine. I should be on top of the world. And yet something keeps nagging at me and I can't make it go away."

She sat down beside him. "Talk about it. Maybe that might help."

He was silent for a while. Finally, he muttered, "Simon Stone. Where is he? What is he doing?"

"Running. Hiding." Rayah shrugged. "After last night,

186

I'd say those were his only options. He doesn't have super-natural powers, Gus."

"No, he's just a man. But, damn it, he's a man who won't quit, not while there's the slightest chance he can do what he set out to do."

She chuckled. "You mean there's more than one of them?"

"Yeah, we're cut from the same cloth. Maybe that's what really worries me. Neither one of us knows when we're licked. And I'm not going to be able to relax until I know he's been put out of commission, one way or another."

"Well, there goes our picnic." Rayah sighed. "Perhaps it's just as well. You'd have been rotten company, anyway."

Fuselli was in his office although, on a normal Saturday, he would not have been. He had, in fact, spent the night there and was on the verge of leaving for home when Gamble's phone call reached him. No, Simon Stone had still not been apprehended. However, he had apparently not fled Rome. The Vatican had received a second threatening letter this morning, this one delivered by messenger.

"Basically, the message is the same as the first," Fuselli said. "With this difference: Because the Pope had the audac-ity to call in the police, he has obstinately set his face against God and will be punished accordingly."

"Um," Gamble said. "What do you make of it?"

"I'm inclined to put it down to braggadocio. Stone has lost his bomb. However, we will be on our guard—in case he has it in his mind to employ a less lethal weapon. No one will be permitted to approach His Holiness close enough to do him harm."

"How about when he appears on the balcony? He'll be a perfect target for a rifle."

"My men will be stationed in and around the piazza, and on the rooftops surrounding it. Furthermore, I've asked for

187

a helicopter to provide aerial surveillance."

His calm professionalism relieved a large part of Gamble's anxiety. "Is there anything you'd like me to do, Colonel?"

"You've already done more than your share. Leave the rest to us. Oh, by the way, we have dismantled Stone's bomb. It was a rather simple device, actually—a core of plutonium encased in TNT. The timer was an ordinary twelve-hour clock, which would allow the person who set it to be out of Rome, even out of the country, before the bomb exploded."

"I'm sure Stone planned to hang around to watch his thunderbolt."

"Well, be that as it may, he won't have that pleasure." Fuselli sighed. "Frankly, I can't comprehend how any man, even a madman, could contemplate such a monstrous act. Our physicists tell me that his bomb was in the one-fifth-kiloton range, enough to obliterate everything within a quarter-mile radius, not to mention the effects of the radioactive fallout. We can consider ourselves fortunate, my friend."

"Yeah, I guess that—" Suddenly, his breath caught in his throat. "Wait a minute, Colonel. How many kilotons did you say?"

"One-fifth, according to the estimate."

"Oh, my God!" Gamble breathed. "Don't you see what that means? A one-fifth-kiloton bomb translates to ten kilos of ploot. But twenty kilos were stolen." His hand that held the receiver was trembling and so was his voice. "So where's the other ten kilos?"

It was all so logical, actually. Once you have the plutonium—and the tools, materials and expertise to fashion it into a weapon—it requires little more effort to make two bombs instead of one. And if your aim is nuclear blackmail, the second is a far more effective lever than the first. Warn your victim that you have an atomic bomb and his reply may well be "Perhaps you do and perhaps you don't. It might be a bluff." But explode the first and then warn, "I have a second"—and, with your credibility no longer in doubt, the victim will be strongly impelled to capitulate. The fear of what may happen is never as strong as the fear of what may happen again. Man, the eternal optimist, bases his life on the assumption that the worst, though possible, will not occur. Shatter that assumption and he begins to tremble.

"Isn't it possible, though," Fuselli argued wearily as he paced up and down his office, "that the missing ten kilos were simply lost in the manufacturing process?"

"Stone wouldn't have been that careless. Besides, we went over the mortuary he used as a workshop with Geiger counters. There was no trace of the stuff. There were two bombs, Colonel. The one we found at San Callisto was the spare."

Fuselli swore with the righteous anger of a man who has believed a difficult job over, only to be told that it is not. "Could it be hidden in the catacomb? Could we have overlooked it?"

"I think not. It makes no sense to hide one and not the other. Stone wasn't expecting to be raided, remember. I believe he took the bomb with him. That's the reason we didn't catch him with the others. He was delivering it to the Vatican."

"Alone?"

"One man could carry the box. One man could go just about anywhere in the Vatican without attracting attention. Especially if he knows his way around—and Stone does. And especially if he was disguised as a priest—which Stone easily could have been. He must have an old robe in his closet."

Fuselli shook his head stubbornly. "For once, your logic is flawed. You're overlooking the timing device, the twelve-hour clock. Unless Simon Stone is a magician, there's no way he could place his bomb on Good Friday and command it to explode on Easter."

"I believe his plan was to slip the bomb into the Vatican early—before a cordon could be established—and then go back to it at the proper time. Our job is to find the bomb before that time. Or, at the very least, to make sure that it and Stone don't get together."

"Do you think we can?" Fuselli wondered gloomily. "The man seems to have the devil's own luck."

"Well, look at it this way, Colonel. If we can't beat the devil in the Holy City—and on Easter—then we're in really deep trouble."

The
Kill

SINCE THE VATICAN is a sovereign state, a nation within a nation, the Roman police have no authority there. Fuselli had to secure special permission before his army could invade the grounds where popes had reigned supreme since 1377. Thanks to the ponderous workings of bureaucracy, it was evening before the search actually got under way.

The task, as Gamble was informed more than once, was staggering. While the city-state was not large—in area it measured less than half a square mile—it offered a formidable choice of possible hiding places. The buildings and palaces presented challenge enough. They ranged from the small post office to the sprawling museum, one of the world's great storehouses of art and statuary, whose library alone contained over a million books and rare manuscripts. Many were several stories in height with cellars and crypts below and towers and cupolas above. Each was, to some extent, a maze of rooms and alcoves and corridors in which even those

191

who worked there sometimes lost their way. Nor could the lush lawns and tree-shaded gardens which occupied roughly half of the grounds be ignored. While logic suggested that the ploot bomb would be hidden in the huge cathedral or adjacent to it, there was no way to be sure. So great was the atom's power that virtually anywhere within Vatican City could be considered Ground Zero.

Each of the five entrances was blocked by armed guards, including the spur rail line on the south. The Holy See—which published its own newspaper, printed its own money and operated its own radio station—also had its own railway station. The walls which dated from the year 800 and the more modern avenues surrounding them were heavily patrolled. But despite this, Vatican City was far from being an impregnable fortress nor was there any feasible way to make it so. Tonight this was the busiest spot in all Rome. Traffic, both vehicular and pedestrian, flowed in and out constantly and would throughout the night as the *famiglia pontifica,* the Pope's personal entourage, made ready for the Pontifical Mass and the other ceremonies surrounding it. The Vatican's normal population numbered nearly a thousand. Now, swelled by dignitaries and their aides from many nations and every order of the Catholic church, it stood at more than twice that figure. It was impossible to deny them access to the shrine. The best the police could do was to demand identification . . . and identification could be forged or stolen.

"We'd better find the bomb," Gamble warned. "It's our best bet."

The search went on. Gamble kept vigil with Fuselli in the command post set up in the Government Palace where (was it only yesterday?) he had held his fruitless discussion with Emilio Mattei, and listened to the reports flowing in from the search teams. Their burden was numbingly repetitive. Academy of Sciences, checked and clear. Mosaic factory, checked and clear. Collegio Etiopico, Sistine Chapel, Belvedere Palace . . . checked and clear.

Midnight came and went. Easter, the eagerly awaited day of resurrection, began, heralded by the bells of Rome's five hundred churches breaking their three-day silence of mourning for the death of Jesus. Soon the triumphal words—"He lives!"—would be pronounced not only here but throughout the world, a signal for rejoicing. The knowledge, far from uplifting Gamble's spirit, filled him with foreboding. Theoretically, at least, the deadly time clock was now running, its hands moving inexorably toward the moment of catastrophe.

"The most ghastly part about it," he fretted, "is that it's pointless. It has been from the beginning. Stone can kill a lot of people, including the Pope, and it won't change a thing. All he can hope for is the satisfaction of revenge, and he won't even be around to enjoy that."

"You believe that he doesn't plan to escape?"

"Why should he? If his doctor is right, Stone is already terminal."

"Well," said Fuselli, patting his pistol significantly, "if death is what he seeks, I'll be glad to accommodate him."

But for a pistol to be employed, a target is required—and the target remained elusive. By five o'clock the inspection of all save two of the buildings had been completed. These were the cathedral and the papal apartments. In the former, the search was already well along. In the latter, it could not begin until the occupant had arisen and departed the premises.

Gamble, unable to sit quietly any longer, left Fuselli at the command post and went outside. Dawn was not far off but the grounds were still shrouded in night and through the darkness moved the flashlights and lanterns of the search teams as they poked into shrubbery and examined the branches of the trees.

193

Looking up, he saw the massive dome of the basilica silhouetted against the lightening sky. It had witnessed over one hundred and twenty-seven thousand sunrises; it seemed inconceivable that this could be its last. And yet in only a few more hours, the mighty cathedral—the work of Michelangelo and Raphael and Bramonte—might be nothing but radioactive dust . . . and the ground on which it stood, where Christ's chief disciple had himself been crucified, poisoned for ages to come.

"Oh, God," he said aloud. "Don't let it happen."

The interior of the basilica was a beehive of activity. Scores of workmen moved among the four hundred columns and past the forty-four altars, making the final preparations for the Easter Mass. The main altar with its incredible baroque canopy which weighed over forty-six tons had been ready since Maundy Thursday when, as custom demanded, it had been washed with wine and balm. But elsewhere there was still much to do. White-robed sextons glided about, checking the placement of the holy vessels and replenishing the votive candles. Down the 700-foot nave and in the slightly shorter transept, the *sampietrini,* the workmen who maintained the cathedral, were assembling the temporary bleachers and arranging the folding chairs on which the privileged would sit. Television technicians in orange coveralls laid cables and tested the flood lamps which the cameras required. And through it all stalked the carabinieri, easily identified even without their uniforms by their ever-moving, always-suspicious eyes.

The doors to the cathedral were closed but outside the faithful had already begun to gather. Some, in fact, had been there for hours, hoping to be among those admitted to witness the Mass which the less fortunate would only hear through the loudspeakers set up in the piazza. Each had been

194

scrutinized by Fuselli's cordon of police but soon, Gamble realized unhappily, the sheer volume of the crowd would render the inspection cursory at best. Yet the worshipers could not be turned away; the possibility had been tentatively broached to the Vatican authorities and emphatically vetoed. This was no soccer match to be canceled or postponed. This was the feast of the glorious Resurrection and would be celebrated on schedule. The Pope himself, informed of the danger, had replied in the words of David, "The Lord is my light and my salvation. Whom shall I fear?"

"He's a brave man," Fuselli conceded. "Unless I'm careful, I may become another Manzù." He referred to the famous Italian sculptor, a dedicated Communist, who had been converted to Catholicism by an earlier pope while working on the cathedral doors. "All the same, does he have the right to ask others to pay the price of his bravery?"

"Every leader does. Including you, Colonel. You're asking your own people to put their lives on the line. Or do you intend to send them all home before noon?"

Fuselli smiled. "The notion did occur to me. But you're right, of course. We all must serve our own particular god, whatever it may be. The Pope has his and I have mine—and neither will permit us to run away like sensible men should." He eyed Gamble curiously. "But what, pray tell, is your excuse?"

That conversation had taken place hours before. Now he sat in the small chapel behind the main altar—where, on all the great festivals of the church, the most holy relics were displayed, including the veil of Veronica and the point of the lance which had pierced the side of Jesus—and he pondered Fuselli's question. He had no official responsibility here, either clerical or secular. Having done his best to save others, he could not be blamed for now attempting to save himself. That being true, why did he refuse to do so? Was it because

195

he, the humble shepherd, felt impelled to remain with the sheep? Or was it because he, the prideful hunter, could not bear to give up the chase? "Will the real Gus Gamble please stand up," he muttered. At this moment, his personal identity crisis was important to no one except himself (and events shortly might render the whole matter academic) but, on what could be the final morning of his life, he felt a desperate urgency to know at last who and what he really was.

And so—although others might have considered it odd—he prayed not for deliverance but for enlightenment.

It had still not come when, shortly after eight o'clock, Fuselli found him. "So this is where you're hiding! I've been looking for you."

"Good news?" Gamble asked hopefully.

"To a certain extent. My men have completed the search and have found nothing."

"I don't see how that can be considered good news to any extent."

"Only in that we can now safely assume that the bomb is not here, after all. That is not to say that Simon Stone still does not intend to deliver it. I'm sure that he does, although in what manner I cannot say. But now that we know our backs are secure, we can concentrate our efforts on making sure that he does not penetrate our perimeter."

To this end, the search teams, their primary mission completed, had been dispatched to reinforce the cordon outside the walls. In the streets which led to Vatican City, already barred to traffic, barricades were being erected to nullify the possibility of a kamikaze attack by truck or automobile. As a further precaution, Fuselli had ordered all private aircraft in the Rome area grounded and decreed the air space over the city off limits to even the commercial carriers.

"You seem to have thought of everything," Gamble agreed.

"Actually, this may be the safest spot in all Rome this morning. Rid yourself of fear, my friend. Immerse yourself in the Mass." Fuselli shrugged. "Those who believe in such mumbo-jumbo tell me that it is quite spectacular."

And spectacular it certainly was. Once the dignitaries had been seated, diplomats and nobility and visiting clergy from around the world, the doors of the cathedral were flung open to admit the less exalted worshipers who rapidly filled the great nave to its twenty thousand capacity. Only a few were lucky enough to find seats. Most were compelled to stand for what, before it was over, would amount to at least two hours. Yet no one complained. For them, this was a rare (perhaps once-in-a-lifetime) opportunity to participate in Christianity's greatest rite performed in Christianity's greatest church.

On the stroke of eleven, the moment for which they patiently waited finally arrived. Heralded by trumpets, the *cappella papale,* the papal entourage, entered the hall. The large procession, consisting of cardinals and bishops, Roman princes, chamberlains and prelates and representatives of the various religious orders plus Knights of Malta and members of the Swiss Guard, marched chanting toward the central altar. Their robes and uniforms and tunics, gold and violet and scarlet and blue, composed a slow-moving river of color made even more dazzling by the neutral backdrop furnished by the cathedral itself.

At the end of this river, last but by no means least, came the Pope. He rode on a throne mounted on a platform, the *sedia gestatoria,* which was borne on the shoulders of a dozen servants. The sedia's cloth-of-silver canopy was supported by eight prelates while, on either side of the throne, a privy chamberlain carried a huge fan festooned with ostrich feathers.

Gamble studied the Pope intently as the throne passed the spot where he stood. The pontiff was one of the few present who was aware of the threat posed by his one-time subordinate, but if it caused him any apprehension it was not reflected on the pale and lined, but still radiant, features. Quite the opposite: The heir to Peter obviously stood in fear of no earthly power.

As the Pontifical High Mass began, Gamble resolved to emulate him. And yet he could not. Although he strove to shut out anxiety and to submerge himself in the ritual, his thoughts continued to wander as restlessly as his eyes which scanned the faces of his fellow worshipers. Fuselli's strategy was sound, his defense meticulously constructed. And still Gamble remembered an armored truck which had been called impregnable, a coffin which no one had thought to open, a subterranean ambush which had failed to net its quarry . . . Had Simon Stone again found a way to outwit them, after all?

The question hammered in his brain, demanding an answer he could not give—until, at last, he was unable to withstand its insistence. It made his participation in the Mass meaningless. He could not celebrate Christ's victory over death while simultaneously fearing its sting.

He edged his way through the crush of worshipers and sought escape via the nearest doorway. The room behind it was empty but, at the end of a short corridor, he found another which was not. Here the television crew had chosen to set up their temporary control booth. A large console, boasting nearly a dozen screens, stood against one wall, monitored by a trio of engineers. Behind them prowled the director, a bushy-haired young man in a plaid shirt and faded levis, snapping his fingers nervously as he selected the shots from the images available to him and giving terse instructions to the cameramen situated in and around the basilica through the telephone headset he wore.

"Number Two, hold the closeup. Number One, stand by for slow zoom. Cue Number Five. Number Four, what the hell's with your focus? You're going soft on me . . ."

Since no one forbade it, Gamble stood and watched, intrigued by the behind-the-scenes glimpse of the electronic marvel in action. At the same time he was wryly amused to realize that, by merely taking a few steps, he would be able to observe the actual ceremony in all its total grandeur instead of two-dimensional fragments selected by another.

The director became aware of his presence. "Yeah?" he asked impatiently. He was a fellow Yankee, not entirely surprising since it was the Knights of Columbus which had provided the funds to broadcast the Mass worldwide by satellite.

"Just watching," Gamble explained.

The director gave him a be-my-guest shrug and went back to business. The Mass was drawing to its close. A moment later, the Pope pronounced the benediction. The *cappella papale* began its slow recess down the length of the cathedral, accompanied by a mighty Te Deum from the choir. The congregation prepared to follow. Shortly, the pontiff would appear on the central balcony high above the piazza from where he would deliver his traditional Easter message.

"Well, that's the tough part," the director observed to no one in particular. "Okay, ready Number Seven. Walter, we'll go to you for the wrap on the Mass in fifteen seconds. I'll need two minutes." On Monitor 7, a gray-haired man— Walter, apparently—nodded and moistened his lips. There was a short silence. Then, as the director snapped his fingers, Walter's face appeared on the largest monitor. He began to speak, summarizing for the viewers what they had just witnessed.

The director didn't listen. "Let's have a camera check."

New images replaced the old on the console, revealing the exterior of the cathedral. One camera, at ground level, pointed at the doorway through which the worshipers inside were commencing to exit. A second, mounted on a tower near the Fontana obelisk in the center of the piazza, was focused on the tapestry-draped but still vacant balcony.

"Where's Ten?" the director demanded, pointing at a screen which remained blank. Although the engineers fiddled with dials and switches, no picture appeared. "Hey, Number Ten! We've lost your video. Do you have power?" He waited for a reply which did not come, then swore. "God almighty! Now even the frigging phone's dead!" He stared at Gamble accusingly as if he were in some manner responsible.

"What's the problem?"

"Beats the hell out of me, babe." Although it was none of Gamble's business, the director welcomed the opportunity to vent his anger. "I got this camera up on the roof—to cut in crowd reaction—and it's picked now to go out on me. Or maybe the bloody paisano decided to take a siesta, I don't know."

He turned back suddenly to the console. "Tell Walter he'll have to stretch. I got trouble. Number Nine, pan the roof." He leaned closer to the monitor as the tower-mounted camera, obedient to his instructions, began a left-to-right survey of the cathedral's roof from which the massive statues of the apostles gazed down benignly on the throng below. "Hold it right there. Give me a zoom." An instant later he swore again, this time more in incredulity than anger.

Gamble stepped forward to peer over his shoulder. Between the statues of Saint Philip and Saint Bartholomew, the malfunctioning camera was plainly visible, its unseeing eye pointed down at the piazza. Equally plain was the fact that it stood untended.

"I can't believe it!" the director said in a strangled voice. "That son of a bitch just walked off and left it. God, I begged them to let me bring in my own people but, no, it had to be local talent—"

Gamble sucked in his breath sharply. He grabbed the director's arm. "Who's the cameraman?"

"How the hell should I know? They're just numbers to me. Besides, he was a last-minute replacement. RAI, the Italian TV people, sent him over to the hotel last night just as the van was leaving. And, brother, are they gonna hear from me!"

"You didn't check with them?"

"I had more important things to do. The creep claimed the first guy'd had an accident or something. I was just happy to have—" The director regarded him apprehensively. "What's with you, buddy? If you're gonna be sick, mind stepping outside? I got enough of a mess here already."

The beads of perspiration on Gamble's suddenly pale face came not from nausea but from the anguish of a man who realizes the truth too late. "Stone told us," he groaned. "It was right there in his letter, plain as day—and I didn't pay any attention. 'The vengeance of God will descend upon you from on high . . .' From on high!"

As he began to run, almost blindly, uncertain of his destination, he recalled that Simon Stone had said something more also. *And the manner of it shall be terrible indeed.* That had been the rest of his promise.

The vast basilica, so crowded only a short time earlier, was nearly empty now. A covey of sextons bustled about the central altar on housekeeping chores and a few worshipers, unwilling to endure the crush outside, lingered to study Michelangelo's Pietà or to kiss the bronze foot of Saint Peter, eroded by countless lips. But the majority had gone to find a vantage point from which to observe the Pope and to hear his Easter message.

Gamble galloped the length of the nave, hoping to spy Fuselli or at least one of his carabinieri. But Fuselli, convinced that the threat must come from outside if it came at all, had withdrawn the last of his guard. He himself had gone with them.

And so, after all, the final responsibility was his and his alone. The duel was between him and Simon Stone; it had been so from the beginning and now must continue to the end. The two men, each a fanatic in his own fashion, had embarked on a collision course from which neither could turn aside. It remained to be seen which—if either—would survive the collision.

A roar from the crowd in the piazza warned that the moment of decision was rapidly approaching. The Pope had appeared on the balcony; shortly, he would begin his message of hope and salvation. How long was the speech to be? Five minutes? Fifteen? Thirty? The answer, Gamble knew, determined the time within which he must achieve victory . . . or accept defeat.

Visitors customarily ascended to the cathedral roof by means of an electric lift. But today the lift was not operating. He sprinted up the stone steps, two or three at a bound. There were seven hundred of them in all; before he reached the midway point, his legs were beginning to cramp and his lungs threatening to burst.

Even at the top there was no time to rest. He plunged into the sunlight, eyes seeking the enemy. The usually busy curio shop was closed and what he could see of the immense roof was empty. Camera Ten still stood untended save by the marble saints. Its operator, the anonymous last-minute replacement, was nowhere to be seen.

202

Gamble circled the huge cupola at a gallop, weaving among the smaller cupolas and towers like a broken field runner, the pounding of his footsteps muffled by the amplified voice of the Pope reverberating from the loudspeakers in the piazza below.

"As all that is within us praises our God for the victory of Easter, what does that victory have to say to us and to our world?"

At every corner he expected to come suddenly face to face with his quarry. But he did not and, when he had finally completed the circuit, he stopped, panting with fatigue and frustration. Had he misinterpreted the cryptic threat, after all? Nowhere in the whole of Vatican City was there a vantage point higher than this maddeningly empty rooftop.

Or was there?

He looked up. Above the massive dome of the cathedral, Michelangelo's last work, rose a conical spire. On its tip, almost seeming to float there, was a gleaming golden ball surmounted by a towering cross. And suddenly he knew. The ball was more than the mere ornament most supposed it to be. It was also an observation point from which, through slits in its side, the privileged visitor might view the entire panorama of the city spread out before him. And from which a crazed prophet, already halfway to heaven, might launch his plutonium thunderbolt on those who scorned him.

"We are called to be the Christ to the prisoner, the poor, the hungry, the hurting masses of this world. We have the message, the resources, the instruction—as well as the command . . ."

Inside the cupola was a second and smaller staircase, barred by a chest-high iron gate. It stood partially open and on the floor lay the ball-peen hammer which had shattered the flimsy lock. Gamble seized it. The hammer was not much of a weapon, puny in comparison to the one held by the enemy, but it was all he had.

He leaped up the winding steps toward the destination he could not see. His feet raised echoes in the narrow staircase, too strident for the distant loudspeakers to conceal. All at once he became aware of a new sound, itself an echo, growing in volume with every step. Simon Stone, unable to hear the pontiff's speech directly, was listening to it on the radio.

"We are promised the power of God's spirit. We know with a deep assurance that because Jesus Christ lives, we too shall live. Truly, abundantly, eternally . . ."

A final turn, and the stairs ended abruptly. He had reached the tip of the spire. Gamble found himself in a tiny windowless chamber, little larger than a closet. From it a steel ladder, anchored to the wall, led to the golden ball itself.

He looked up. From the narrow aperture another face gazed down at him.

The hunter and the hunted stared at each other for a moment in silence. The one had pursued the other halfway around the world, from California desert to this ancient city, implacable antagonists who had never met. Gamble knew Simon Stone only from a photograph. The face he beheld now bore only a passing resemblance to it. The once-handsome features were bloated by the disease which ravaged him and the skin which covered it was gray, made even more so by the vivid orange coveralls he wore. But there was no mistaking the dark magnetic gaze. The long chase was over. This was the enemy.

The realization was mutual. As Gamble put a foot on the ladder, Stone advised, "Don't come any farther." The warning was reinforced by the pistol in his hand.

"I'm not armed," Gamble lied. He kept the hammer close to his side, hoping it could not be seen from above. "I just want to talk to you."

"Certainly," Stone agreed. "But I'm rather busy right now. Come back in a few minutes." He smiled significantly. "Shall we say five?"

He had set the timer. Gamble kept panic from his voice; he took a cautious step upward. "The Pope sent me. He got your letter. He wants to meet you and discuss it."

"You're lying, of course. Not that it matters. There's nothing to discuss. The Bishop of Rome has heard the judgment of God revealed through his servant. He has chosen to ignore it. For that he must be chastised."

On the radio, the Pope's voice intoned, "Lord of life, we need your resurrecting power in these days when the power of death still threatens us so terribly . . ."

"Think about those other people out there," Gamble said. "Did God tell you to chastise them, too?" He took another step.

"The sheep must suffer for the sins of the shepherd in order that righteousness shall be restored." The thousands who stood unknowingly on the brink of death, with more thousands to follow, held no meaning for him. He condemned them with a phrase.

"But why should anyone suffer? You've delivered the Lord's message, Simon. Now give us the chance to heed it."

"I gave you your chance. You rejected me. I spoke to you and you would not listen."

"You're wrong. That's what I'm trying to tell you. The Pope is going to meet your demands. I've read his speech. He's going to end it by hailing you as Simon, the new Peter, the rock on which we will rebuild the church!"

No sane man would believe the preposterous statement. He could only pray that Stone, who was far from sane, might find it credible. At least, for a moment; he was nearly close enough to . . .

"You're lying," Stone said again but, for the first time,

205

there was a note of uncertainty in his voice.

"Disarm the bomb," Gamble urged. "Turn up your radio and listen. Hear for yourself what—"

What they heard was a muffled roar. It came from the crowd in the piazza. A moment later, the announcer's hushed voice said, "And with an appeal for men everywhere to rededicate their lives to the establishment of God's kingdom here on earth, the Pope's Easter message has come to a close. His Holiness is now blessing the huge throng kneeling here in the piazza of Saint Peter's . . ."

Stone stared down at him, more in sorrow than in anger. "Eyes have they and see not," he whispered. "They have ears and hear not." He raised his own eyes toward heaven. "Father, Thy will be done."

Gamble lunged upward. His hand closed on the other man's wrist. In the same instant, the pistol fired. The bullet struck his left shoulder, knocking him off the ladder. But even as he fell, he kept his desperate grip. The two men plunged together the dozen feet to the floor below.

Gamble struggled to his knees, his dazed eyes seeking the enemy. The gun, he thought, got to get the gun. But he couldn't find it and there was no need for it, anyway. He had landed on his back; his body had absorbed the jarring impact. Simon Stone, jerked from his perch above, had landed on his head. He lay face down, one leg doubled beneath him. The other twitched once, then was still.

He had won the fight but the war was far from over. The bomb and not the man was the real enemy. He staggered to his feet. As he did so, he became aware for the first time of his wound. Pain stabbed him like a red-hot spear, making him reel. He tried to steady himself against the wall and found that he could not move his left arm. Blood was trickling down his hand, a hand that, oddly, still clutched the head of the ball-peen hammer. He told himself to drop the

206

useless tool but when he looked down again the hammer was still there. His fingers refused to open.

He forgot about it. The hammer could be disposed of later —if there was to be a later. He grasped the ladder with his good hand. The rungs seemed much farther apart now; to move from one to the next required all his strength. Twice the effort nearly made him faint. Each time he clung to the ladder until his head cleared, then forced his shaking legs to mount to the next step. Or was he only imagining that he was doing so? Whenever he looked up, the top appeared no nearer than before.

But then there came a time when his fingers, groping for the next rung, failed to find it. He puzzled about this for a moment until the significance of it occurred to him. He had reached the top of the ladder. He was inside the golden ball.

The ball was merely golden on the outside. Inside, it was a tarnished gray and the only gold was provided by the sunlight slanting through the slits in the metal skin. One of the narrow bands of light, like a pointing finger, directed his eyes to the oblong steel box.

He could not reach it from the ladder. When he took a step toward it, the curved floor robbed him of what little balance he still possessed. He fell heavily. He was content to lie there, embracing the pillow and allowing the delicious lethargy to engulf him. But the pillow was strangely uncomfortable; he discovered that it was encased by steel rather than linen. His head was resting on the box.

The realization jerked him back to awareness. He forced himself to sit up. The curved wall began to revolve around him like a slow-moving carousel. He commanded it to stop and was gratified when it obeyed. But he knew it was only a temporary victory. Shock and loss of blood were stealing his consciousness as they had stolen his strength and, ulti- mately, not even his terrible tenacity could prevent them.

The lid of the box was closed. He fumbled with the catch and, for one awful moment, believed that it was locked. The key, if any, was in Simon Stone's pocket. For all the chance he had of reaching it, it might as well be on the moon. Then, miraculously, the lid moved.

As with the first bomb, the timing device reposed in the lid. His failing eyes saw but could not read the dial. It seemed to him that the hands stood nearly at twelve; shortly the larger hand would eclipse the smaller.

There must be some way to turn the damned thing off, he thought. Fuselli's bomb squad would know. But they were not here. Only he was here and if there was a cutoff switch his numb fingers could not find it. In despair he pounded on the clock face. The glass resisted the feeble blows. This final injustice made him whimper. He had come so far, overcoming criminal cunning and bureaucratic bungling, defying both church and state, surviving the strangler's noose and the fanatic's bullet . . . only to be defeated in the end by a small clock.

And then he remembered the hammer. Had he dropped it? No, it was still there, tightly clutched by his useless hand. The fingers, convulsed in spasm, surrendered it reluctantly. All his remaining strength was needed to raise it. For just an instant, he hesitated. He had never heard of disarming a bomb by smashing its timing device. For all he knew, the action might well produce the same dreadful consequences he sought to prevent. Yet there was no time to weigh the alternatives. There was, in fact, no alternative; only the width of a hair separated the two hands of the clock.

"What the hell," he said aloud. Odd words in which to couch a prayer but a prayer it was, nonetheless.

He brought the hammer crashing down.

The story furnished later to the news media was a carefully laundered version of the truth, as such stories too frequently are. A bomb threat had been received by the Vatican. Special security measures had been employed; the threat had come to nothing. Since the press takes little interest in false alarms, the matter was briefly noted and quickly forgotten.

The drama ended without applause from an audience which had been unaware of the performance. The actors dispersed, some to accept other roles, the rest to vanish into limbo.

Simon Stone and his four confederates were buried, for lack of a more suitable site, in the American military cemetery at Nettuno. There were no services.

Colonel Ugo Fuselli was given a commendation and promised a promotion. However, official gratitude is ephemeral and he did not receive it. Disgusted, he left the police to enter politics where he crusaded vigorously against the construction of nuclear power plants in Italy. The following year an American environmental group with similar views invited him to a conference in New York. Due to his political persuasion, he was denied a visa.

Rayah Zaparov, the Mossad agent, was recalled to Israel. Her imprudent involvement with a foreign national had stamped her as unreliable. She visited Gamble every day in the hospital before she left. Both promised to write. Neither kept the promise. Later, he heard that she had remarried.

General Ashley Womack retired with a polite "Dear Ash" letter from the President which thanked him for his long service but, significantly, did not urge him to extend it. Six months after, he suffered a stroke and died within a week, leaving his memoirs barely begun.

Kenneth Neff resigned from the Nuclear Regulatory Commission, citing reasons of health. However, he made a remarkable recovery; within the month, he rejoined the CIA where he was assigned to the covert operations section. In an in-house shakeup the following year, he was named assistant to the deputy director, supplanting his sometime friend Nils Berryman.

Otto Lanz used the incident to urge the IAEA to increase the size and scope of his department. The request was refused due to the agency's chronic shortage of funds. Lanz did not press the issue. Ever the practical politician, he sensed that to do so might place his own job in jeopardy.

Gamble's recuperation was slow. The bullet had shattered his shoulder, leaving his left arm partially and permanently paralyzed. When at last he was able to fly home, he had a long talk with Francis Inman.

"I've been offered Womack's job," Gamble told him. "With more authority than the General ever had. But it means leaving the priesthood. What should I do, Father Frank?"

"What do you want to do, Gus?"

"Eat my cake and have it too, I guess. God knows I'm a pretty shabby excuse for a priest. But if the church can forgive my trespasses, I might eventually be able to get it right."

"With repentance—and considering your accomplishments—I believe that forgiveness is likely." Inman smiled. "Even in the church, nothing succeeds like success."

"On the other hand, I enjoy the excitement of police work. If you're good at it—and I am—it can be a marvelous ego trip. Still, that wasn't enough for me once. I'm not sure it ever will be."

"If I hear you correctly," Inman said thoughtfully, "what you want is for your life to have more meaning than you've found as either a priest or a policeman."

"That's about it. But I can't have it both ways. I have to make a choice."

Inman was silent for a while. "I wonder if you really do," he said finally.

"I've tried wearing two hats, Father Frank. It doesn't work."

"How about a third hat—a combination of both?"

"There ain't no such animal."

"Isn't there? For better or worse, we've unlocked the atom. Whether we should or shouldn't have done so is academic now. We've done it. It's foolish to suppose that we can or will lock it up again. Mankind is going to have to live with it. We can use it for good or for evil. It can enrich our lives immeasurably or destroy them utterly. It's an awesome challenge. I'm wondering if God isn't calling you and men like you—men with extraordinary gifts—to meet the challenge. Not just to play policemen but to become a peculiar sort of priesthood, keepers of this new flame. Would that role give your life the meaning it seeks, Gus?"

"The plutonium priesthood," Gamble mused. "It sounds exciting—and terrifying. I'm not certain I can handle the responsibility."

"Someone has to try. Unless you believe that Simon Stone was only an aberration—and that what nearly happened in Rome can never happen again."

Gamble shook his head slowly. "Simon Stone wasn't even the first. He simply came the closest so far. By the end of this century, we'll have produced several hundred thousand pounds of weapons-grade ploot. A lot of maniacs are going to try to get their hands on it. We'd better pray that we can stop them." He sighed. "And work like hell to make sure our prayers are answered."

"Amen," said Francis Inman.